The
Bookshop
Girl

For my nephew Theo: Welcome!

—S. B.

Published by
PEACHTREE PUBLISHERS
1700 Chattahoochee Avenue
Atlanta, Georgia 30318-2112
www.peachtree-online.com

Text © 2017 by Sylvia Bishop
Illustrations © 2018 by Poly Bernatene

First published in Great Britain in 2017 by Scholastic Children's Books,
an imprint of Scholastic Ltd
First United States version published in 2018 by Peachtree Publishers

The illustrations were rendered digitally.

Printed in July 2018 by LSC Communications in Harrisonburg, VA
10 9 8 7 6 5 4 3 2 1
First Edition

ISBN: 978-1-68263-045-7

Library of Congress Cataloging-in-Publication Data

Names: Bishop, Sylvia, author. | Bernatene, Poly, illustrator.
Title: The bookshop girl / written by Sylvia Bishop ; illustrated by Poly Bernatene.
Description: First edition. | Atlanta, Georgia : Peachtree Publishers, 2018. | "First published in the
United Kingdom in 2017 by Scholastic Children's Books, an imprint of Scholastic Ltd."—Title page
verso. | Summary: Property Jones and her family are in dire straits when they win a drawing for
the greatest bookstore in England but the previous owner was hiding something nearly as big as
Property's secret.
Identifiers: LCCN 2017047030 | ISBN 9781682630457
Subjects: | CYAC: Bookstores—Fiction. | Family life—England—Fiction. | Literacy—Fiction. |
Secrets—Fiction. | Swindlers and swindling—Fiction. | Foundlings—Fiction. | England—Fiction.
Classification: LCC PZ7.1.B553 Boo 2018 | DDC [Fic]—dc23 LC record available at *https://lccn.loc.
gov/2017047030*

The Bookshop Girl

Sylvia Bishop

Illustrated by Poly Bernatene

Ω

PEACHTREE
ATLANTA

Contents

Before We Begin

You have in your hands the story of Property Jones. I hope that your copy smells of something nice—like crisp, new paper, or that churchy secondhand-book smell, or some lemonade that someone spilled on it once.

There's a lot of story to tell, so we should get started. But the trouble with a name like "Property Jones" is that people are very bothered by it, and before you can begin the story they want to know whether Property is a girl's name or a boy's name and whether Property can really be a name at all and what Jones has to do with it. So I will quickly explain.

Property Jones was left in a bookshop when she was five years old. Her parents walked out and left her there—just like that. She was found by Michael Jones, who was ten at the time and who dutifully put her in the lost property cupboard.

When Netty saw this, she sighed in a sensible sort of way. Netty was Michael's mother and owned the bookshop and was an altogether sensible sort of person.

"People aren't property, Michael," she explained. "You can't put a girl in a cupboard."

But he obviously could because he had, and Property was too little and too confused to come out of the cupboard or to tell anyone anything useful like her name. Netty called the police and put up posters and so on. But nobody ever came for Property.

In the end, she just stayed. She came out of the cupboard, but she never did tell them her name. These days, I don't think she even remembers it. They tried to come up with a new one for her, but Property was the only thing that stuck.

The three of them lived together in the bookshop, which is an odd thing to do, but they didn't have anywhere else to go. And besides, they liked it there. Anyway, that is the tale of how Property Jones came by the name Property and how she became a Jones. Now, take the next page between your finger and thumb...and turn it. We can start.

Chapter One
An Object of Wonder

Property was eleven years old when our story begins. She had been living with the Joneses for six years. She loved them very much, and she was almost entirely happy there. But she was never *completely* happy because she was keeping a secret from them, and it was a whopper:

Property Jones couldn't read.

Every evening, Netty and Michael would take two copies of the same book and read them side by side, turning the pages at the same time and laughing and sighing at all the same parts. When it had become clear that Property was staying, Netty had given her a third copy each night without a word.

She was trying to be kind. It never occurred to Netty that the five-year-old newcomer might not be able to read. And it was a long time before it occurred to

Property that the others weren't just admiring the books and enjoying the weight and smell of them and the way the pages rustled. So at first, she just copied what they were doing and didn't know that anything was wrong.

Once she realized that she had misunderstood, she was too scared to say anything in case they threw her out. Of course, when she was older, she realized that this was silly, but by then she had pretended to read for so long that it seemed very dishonest, and she was ashamed to tell them. And as she got older and older, this went on longer and longer, and it got more and more awkward, and now she had pretended to be able to read for six whole years.

And that is why, when Netty read something in the paper that made her raise her eyebrows in surprise and then passed it to Michael, who fell out of his chair in surprise before passing it to Property, Property didn't know what it said. She searched for a reaction somewhere in between eyebrow-raising and falling-off-a-chair, and said, "Oh!" This seemed to satisfy them.

"It's a miracle," said Michael from underneath the counter.

"Not a miracle, Michael," said Netty. "Just—wonderful."

Michael explained that this was exactly what he

meant, and that the word "miracle" comes from the Latin *miraculum* which means "object of wonder." This was quite clever, but the others weren't particularly impressed. First, Michael always knew that kind of thing. Second, he was still sitting foolishly under the counter.

"The real miraculum," said Netty, "is that I ever run a shop with you two for help. Out from under the counter, Michael. It's two minutes to nine."

So Michael came out, still beaming about the mysterious Object of Wonder in the newspaper, and they all took up their places. They always worked the same way. Netty sat at the counter to serve the customers. She used it as a desk as well, to do all the difficult things like finances and ordering stock. Michael took care of the books, lovingly arranging them on the shelves and recommending his favorites to people, whether or not they wanted him to. There weren't that many books in the shop, and a lot of them were yellow or wrinkly with age, but Michael loved them anyway.

Property served tea and cake to anyone who wanted to sit in an armchair and read awhile, and she kept the shop smart and tidy. Or she tried to. It didn't help that everything in the shop was falling apart.

Netty was at the counter, Michael was hovering by the dictionaries, and Property had put the kettle on. The White Hart opened at nine o'clock sharp. (If you are thinking, *But the White Hart is the wrong sort of name for a bookshop*, then you are quite right, but also quite impatient. I was going to explain. The bookshop used to be the White Hart pub, and it had a very beautiful picture of a white stag hanging outside. When Netty bought the pub and filled it with books, she couldn't see any good reason to change the name when there was such a nice sign already there.)

It was a slow day. Whenever the shop was quiet, Netty and Michael would talk about the Object of Wonder, and Property would try to figure out what it was.

"Of course," said Netty, wrapping her hands tightly around her mug of tea, "it will never be us. The chance is so slim."

"Of course," agreed Michael. "We shouldn't even think about it." But then he put out a batch of thriller books upside down, so either he thought they looked better that way or he was still thinking about it. (Property could tell that they were thrillers easily; it was just a matter of paying attention. They had dark, moody covers, and they were the right sort of fatness with thinnish paper. Whenever Netty and Michael read books that looked like that, their breathing was very tense.)

Michael finally noticed what he was doing and turned all the books the right way up. Then he said, "It would be amazing though. I've heard it's huge! We'd have every book in the world." And his face lit up at this beautiful thought.

"And no trouble paying the gas bill," said Netty, looking sadly at her hot cup of tea. The White Hart was always a *little* bit too cold.

Property leaned closer to her own mug of tea, feeling the warmth on her face. She was used to playing detective, but this was a tough case. What could hold every book in the world and heat up their shop? Was there some sort of infinity shelf fitted with its own radiator system? She got a bit lost imagining what this would look like and accidentally leaned right into the tea and scalded her chin. A woman browsing the cookbook section gave her a very strange look. Property quickly put the tea down and hurried off to look busy with a vacuum.

As she was vacuuming, she eavesdropped some more.

"Have you entered us yet?" Michael was saying.

"Of course," said Netty. "I did it right away."

"I wonder if there are runner-up prizes," said Michael. "I'd love to just *meet* him." Michael had a face shaped like a pear, mostly taken up with eyes, and those eyes were now getting bigger and bigger and bigger. Whatever was going on, it must be good. The only thing that normally made Michael this excited was a really good dictionary full of especially interesting words. (Property could tell that a book was a dictionary from the paper—so thin that she could trace with it—and the tiny writing, and the boring covers without any pictures).

Netty smiled at him. "You do choose odd heroes, love. The great Albert H. Montgomery himself, eh? Sure, it would be nice."

This was more intriguing by the minute. Albert H. Montgomery owned the greatest bookshop in Britain. Probably in the world. Property didn't know anyone who had actually seen the Montgomery Book Emporium, which was miles away in London, but everybody had heard of it. There was a rumor that the Queen herself bought all her books from Montgomery's.

But what did the Book Emporium have to do with their heating bill? Property casually vacuumed the same spot for ten minutes while she thought this one over and didn't even notice that she was vacuuming her own foot.

The cookbook woman was now looking at Property as if she was quite worried about her.

That afternoon it rained, so the shop was rammed full. Something about a good hard downpour makes every-body suddenly remember how much they'd like to buy a book, especially if they happen to have forgotten their umbrella. The three armchairs at the front of the shop were full, and the window seat in the fantasy section was full, and every possible nook and cranny had someone huddled in it.

Property was not used to the shop being this full, and she didn't like it. It was difficult to move anywhere without knocking something or someone over. Worse still, it meant that there were too many customers for Netty and Michael to deal with, so some people would try to ask Property questions that she couldn't possibly answer.

"Excuse me," said a fiercely eyebrowed woman, catching Property's elbow through the crowd. She was a regular at the White Hart, and she was the least fun person ever. "Do you have any books on quadratic equations with complex roots?"

"Er," said Property, wondering what a quadratic equation was and how to avoid meeting one, "I'll just

check." And she tried to push through the throng to ask Michael, but someone in the crowd stumbled into her and knocked her into the umbrella stand, which spilled its umbrellas all over the floor. While she was picking them up, a solemn young man tapped her on the shoulder.

"Little girl," he said, "do you have anything by Wordsworth? It's rather urgent." He clasped his hands together and stared at her sadly. "His poetry is medicine for the heart, and mine is very heavy."

"Right—er—sorry to hear it," said Property. "Poetry's over there." And before he could ask her to look for a specific book, she hurried off to sit on top of the Art and Photography shelf. Netty had fixed this shelf to the wall especially, so that it wouldn't topple over when they sat on it, and had put some cushions on top. It was one of Property's favorite places. She tucked herself into the corner and made herself as small as possible, so that she wouldn't have to deal with any more heavy hearts or complex roots or umbrella stands. She took the newspaper up there with her to see if she could find any clues in it.

When Michael joined her a few minutes later, she tried her most desperate trick, which she only used on special occasions. She handed him the newspaper. "Read it out, Michael," she said. "I want to hear it out loud." And she tried to look full of wonder, which is difficult when you are concentrating on not falling off a bookcase.

So Michael pushed his glasses up his nose, and *aherrmed* a bit, and began:

CALLING ALL BOOK LOVERS!

Could YOU be the next owner of the Great Montgomery Book Emporium?

Albert H. Montgomery is retiring and has chosen to offer his world-famous bookshop as a once-in-a-lifetime prize!

For the chance to win, simply enter
The Grand Montgomery Drawing!
The lucky winner will be announced on
Saturday, October 31st.

Hurry—enter now for your chance to win
yourself a Book Emporium!

Visit *www.montgomerybookemporium.com*
There are literally no terms or conditions.

While he was reading, Netty had climbed up the ladder with two more mugs of tea—which is quite clever, if you stop and think about it. She set down one for each of them. "Listen to you two nattering! We all need to stop jittering about it. We're so unlikely to win." She ran a finger along the top row of books. They coughed up a cloud of dust, and a paperback on the end fell apart. "We've got our own emporium right here anyway," she said. But she didn't sound like she believed it.

As she watched her mum get gobbled up by the crowd on the shop floor, Property didn't know what to feel. It was certainly a wonderful prize, but the thought of leaving home was surprisingly painful. "So if we won," she said, "would we leave the White Hart?"

Michael looked at her properly. He was the kind of person who often looked without *really* looking because he was busy thinking about a puzzle or a really interesting word. But he could tell when somebody actually needed his attention.

"I know that wouldn't be easy, Prop," he said. He hugged his knees up to his chest and lowered his voice. "But we might have to do it anyway, drawing or no drawing. This place has been in a bad way for a while. Mum's not letting on. I only know 'cause I go over the accounts when she's not looking and correct a few of the sums—I've always done it, she never notices. Anyway. You might not have realized, Prop, but the bookshop isn't making nearly enough money."

Property looked at her brother, who blinked earnestly back at her. Michael could be very stupid for a very clever person. The White Hart was cold, broken, and badly stocked. Property was wearing Michael's old clothes, and Michael was in clothes that were much too small. Netty's nice jewelry had disappeared piece by piece until she had nothing left to sell, and she kept ramming her pen fiercely into the page whenever she did their accounts and making endless tea to calm herself down. But Michael only knew that they were in trouble because he had done some math. Sometimes, Property felt she was the only Jones that paid any attention.

It was difficult to think how to reply. Luckily, Netty appeared over the top of the bookcase with two more steaming mugs. "More tea?"

Her children looked at their full mugs. "All right up here, thanks, Mum," said Property. And she decided to want the Book Emporium for Netty's sake.

Of course, however much any of them wanted it, there was nothing to do but wait. There were two nights until the drawing. That first night, none of them slept very well. As Property fidgeted in her hammock, she could hear the others fussing about in their own hammocks in their own corners of the shop. Netty Jones slept in the secondhand section because she liked the musty smell of the old books. Michael slept by the dictionaries because he liked things to say exactly what they meant. Property slept in the travel section because travel books have pictures.

The next day it didn't rain, so nobody remembered that they wanted to buy a book. While the Joneses waited to find out if they had won the world's largest book emporium, they sold a grand total of three novels. Netty made record amounts of tea and accidentally snapped her pen in half.

They *did* have people in the shop—lots of people—but they only came in to talk with Netty about the Grand Montgomery Drawing and swap rumors about the Emporium. None of them had been to London, so they were really just guessing. Some people had heard it was a hundred stories high, and some had heard it was built entirely of marble, and one rather excitable man had heard that it was staffed by highly trained leopards. The least-fun-woman-ever had heard that all of its books were in Latin and none of them had pictures. But all of these people had one thing in common: they had entered the drawing, and they wanted to win.

The morning of the drawing was overbrimming with that glad sort of wintry sunlight that you only see a few times a year. The street glowed outside the shop window. It was such hopeful weather that the Joneses couldn't help feeling like they just might win.

"Of course," said Netty sensibly, "the weather is the same for everyone." And they all nodded. But Property's heart didn't slow down. She wondered how the winner would be chosen. Was Albert H. Montgomery himself pulling names out of a hat this very minute?

There was a sharp trill.

The Joneses looked about the shop in confusion before they realized that this was what their telephone sounded like. Property tried to remember if anyone had ever called it before. Netty picked it up, and Property noticed that her hand was shaking slightly.

"Hello?" she said.

A sophisticated sort of warble came from the phone.

"Yes, speaking," said Netty.

There was more sophisticated warbling. Netty sat down heavily on the counter.

"Oh!" she said. Property's heart went into overdrive. "I—oh! I can't believe it!"

Warblewarblefancywarble.

"Yes, of course! Thank you so much!"

Netty Jones put down the phone and looked up at her two children. "An Object of Wonder," she said faintly. And then suddenly Michael was hugging Property, and Property was hugging Netty, and Netty was hugging Michael, until they all got tangled up into one big hug that was just hugging itself.

From somewhere in the middle of the hug, Netty's voice broke free. "Come on, come on, enough nonsense." And she laughed, even though nothing was funny. "We've got a lot to do; there's no time to lose. Albert H. Montgomery himself wants to meet us *tomorrow*."

By noon the next day, the White Hart was empty. The first things to go were the books, which the Joneses pushed for free into the arms of willing customers and unwilling customers and startled passersby. The second thing to go was the smell of books. Some cleaners came and replaced it with the smell of vacuuming and lemon-scented sprays. Then, finally, the Joneses went too.

Netty marched out happily without a pause.

"Goodbye, White Hart," Michael said, turning back at the door. And Property suddenly wanted to crawl right back inside her cupboard and never say goodbye. Goodbye seemed very final. It meant that they really weren't going to return.

When she said this, though, Michael just told her firmly that "goodbye" is short for "God be with ye," so it doesn't mean anything about not returning. This was not even a little bit useful, but it cheered Property up anyway. It was good to know that, whatever happened, Michael would carry on being Michael. So Property took a deep breath, got a lung full of the lemon smell, coughed, picked up her suitcase, and followed her brother out of their shop.

The three of them caught a fast train to London. At six o'clock, while the White Hart stood in darkness with nobody to turn on the lights, the Joneses arrived at the Montgomery Book Emporium.

Chapter Two

The Great Montgomery Book Emporium

It was dark when the Joneses arrived at their new home. There was a huge shadow on the steps, which turned out to be a crowd of reporters waiting to meet them. The Grand Montgomery Drawing, it seemed, was national news.

As the Joneses approached, the reporters began shouting out questions. Michael helpfully tried to answer all of them, while Netty said more sensible things like, "Excuse me," and, "Sorry, could we get through please?" and, "Ow!" (when somebody jostled them especially hard).

"How does it feel?" shouted someone, and, "Where are you from?" yelled another. One woman grabbed Property by the arm. "Little girl!" she squawked. "Tell the nation: What's your favorite book?"

Lying to the Joneses was hard enough; Property didn't want to have to lie to the whole nation. So she said,

"EXCUSE ME!" extra-loudly, stuck out her elbows, pushed her way to the front, and rang the bell.

The door swung open at once with a sigh. The three of them stepped inside, and it swung shut behind them. Everything was suddenly silent.

The room that they entered was round, with dark wooden walls and a soft carpet and a beautiful marble ceiling very high above them. It was full of sleepy armchairs and quiet lamps. It felt exceptionally bookshop-ish—only... there didn't seem to be any shelves of books.

As Property's eyes adjusted to the lamplight, she saw that there were a dozen mahogany doors spaced evenly around the room—thirteen, if you counted the front door as well. She supposed that the books must be behind the doors. The whole place *smelled* of books, anyway, so they had to be nearby.

"Oh," said Netty in delight. "*Oh.*" And Property was inclined to agree. She hadn't been so warm in years.

"Yes, *oh,* indeed," said an armchair. With a start, Property realized that the armchair had a man in it. He was dressed in the same plum-colored velvet as the chair, and he had a soft, ruddy face, with a most magnificent mustache. He smiled at them. "Also *ahh,* I find, especially when the rain falls on the roof." He stood up and

stretched his arms out to match his stretched-out smile. "Welcome, my dear Joneses, to the *Great Montgomery Book Emporium!*"

Netty and Property both said, "Thank you," and, "Hello," and so on. Michael did an odd little bow because meeting Albert H. Montgomery himself had made him feel particularly awkward. His glasses fell off. Montgomery generously pretended not to notice.

"You must be Netty Jones," he said to Netty. "Splendid. And you two...?" He turned to Property and Michael, all spread-out smile and spread-out hands.

Michael was busy trying to remember how to function, so Property said that he was Michael and she was Property. This made Montgomery blink a bit (although he never dropped the smile), so Property quickly explained about Michael putting her in the cupboard. Michael found his voice again and *very* quickly explained that this was a long time ago. Montgomery just blinked and smiled and nodded as if this all made a lot of sense.

"Naturally, yes," he said. "I daresay we've all put the odd person in a cupboard in our time. Splendid, splendid. Now, won't you all have some refreshments?" He waved a hand at some of the armchairs, and the Joneses sank obediently into them, while Montgomery passed around lemonade and angel food cake. Nobody wanted angel food cake when the Emporium was waiting to be explored, but they all took a piece to be polite.

"Now," he said, arranging himself back into his arm-chair, "Now, now, *now*. Tell me about yourselves. Are you very fond of books?"

Property was, but probably not in the way he meant, so she left this to the others. But before they could answer, a ball of gray fluff fell from a lamp above and attacked Michael's scalp.

"Gunther," said Montgomery, "*NO.*"

HssssMaaaAAWR, said the cannonball of fluff that was called Gunther.

"*Owowowowow!*" said Michael several times.

Thankfully the fluff soon got bored of scalping Michael, flumped off his head to the floor via his knees, and glared at the new arrivals. It seemed to be a kitten, but it was difficult to be sure. Its head was monstrously big, and its face was so squashed in that its nose was level with its eyes.

"This is one of the famous Gunthers—Gunther Arma-geddon the Third, to be exact" said Montgomery proudly. "They are a very fine family of Persian Blues. This little chap is only eight weeks old."

The Gunther eyed them all grimly, then shot up into Property's lap. She braced herself, but he didn't attack. He just sat and glared at her, squash-faced, unblinking.

"There!" said Montgomery. "He likes you! Splendid! He can't come with me, so he's all yours."

He said this as if the Joneses should be pleased. They all looked at the cat a bit doubtfully.

"And speaking of things that are all yours," Montgomery went on, "would you like to look around this *magnificent* bookshop?"

And they all said that they would, apart from the Gunther, who hissed and crossed his eyes. Property didn't speak cat, but she guessed that this was probably a "no." But the kitten was outnumbered, so they all got up to take the tour, the Gunther hitching a ride on Property's head. Property's heart beat a little faster. What was it like, behind those doors?

"What would you like to see?" asked Montgomery. "Detective novels? Romance novels? War novels? Knights and castles? Cops and robbers? Desert islands? Space adventures? Woodland tales? Bedtime stories? Cookbooks? Dictionaries? Books to use as doorstops? Sticky endings? Sappy endings? Fairies, witches, wizards, dragons? Pirate stories? Ghost stories? Stories about the ghosts of pirates?"

25

Montgomery paused to breathe in. "That's just the beginning, my dears. That's just a *taste*. Ask for anything at all. I guarantee we have it."

Property tried to imagine the size of the hallways beyond the twelve doors. It made her head hurt just to think about it. Then she realized that her head was mainly hurting because the Gunther was batting at it repeatedly with his front paws. But still: that was a lot of books.

Michael chose first. "Please—could we see the dictionaries?"

"Aha," said Montgomery, "a man after my own heart. A very fine choice." And he walked to one of the doors. Where there should have been a door handle, there was a brass lever. He pulled it down.

There was a tremendous roar. It sounded as if the whole bookshop had a bellyache and they were trapped somewhere in its gut. Property wasn't sure whether this was *meant* to happen, but the Gunther started yowling in delight, so she guessed that it was probably normal. It went on for an awful ten seconds, then stopped. Montgomery opened the door.

Property expected more dark wood and lamplight, but the room inside was white and well lit. The books were arranged in strict, straight lines, and each had a brown tag attached. Actually, *everything* in the room had a brown tag attached. Property looked at the nearest one, on the inside doorknob. It was covered in small, boring black type.

"In the Room of Dictionaries," said Montgomery, "everything has a definition. Not the most beautiful room, perhaps, but very satisfying. Wouldn't you say so, young Michael?"

Young Michael couldn't reply, because his jaw had dropped on discovering so many dictionaries at once, and he was having trouble getting it back again.

Montgomery gave it a moment, then said, "Splendid. Yes, well. Perhaps you'd like to pick a room, young Property?"

Property was thoroughly befuddled. She was still trying to make sense of the bellyache noise and the lever and where all the other rooms could be if there was only one behind each door. But Montgomery was waiting, so she said the first thing that came into her head. "Space adventures, please."

"*Oho*," said Montgomery, "that's in the same stack. Splendid." And he shut the door of the Room of Dictionaries and pulled the lever. Once again, the Emporium and the Gunther groaned and yowled in duet. Then they stopped, and Montgomery opened the door a second time.

The Room of Dictionaries had gone. In its place was a new room, painted all over in deep indigo, speckled with twinkling lights. The books were hanging from fine threads, so that they almost seemed to be floating in midair.

"The Room of Space Adventures," said Montgomery. "I'm rather proud of this one."

"But..." said Netty, as sensibly as she could manage.

"*Whaaa*, er?" Michael asked.

"Where did the other room go?" said Property.

"A*ha*!" said Montgomery. "O*ho*," he added. "Ee*hee*," he tried, to see if that would sound good too. It didn't. So he coughed, embarrassed, and explained how the Great Montgomery Book Emporium worked.

"This Emporium," he said, "this beautiful Emporium is the world's first and only mechanical bookshop. It is my own invention!" He beamed at them. "Consider, my dear Joneses, how an elevator works: one little room, which can be moved up or down. Yes? Well, each of these levers moves a whole *set* of rooms, and not just up and down—they move in a loop: down from the ceiling where they meet the door, then under the shop floor and back up again, like a Ferris wheel. Pull the lever—turn the rooms. You see?"

"I call each loop full of rooms a *stack*. There are twelve stacks—one for each door. Think of that, eh? Think of the *size* of it!" He traced circles in the air with his arms, splashing lemonade everywhere. "This shop floor is right at the heart of it all, my dears. The rest of the bookshop is *all around us*. It's just waiting to be called."

Property and Michael were speechless. Luckily, Netty had all sorts of sensible questions and did the talking for them. Montgomery explained to her about getting the customers to line up for the rooms, and warned her not to let anyone get stuck in the stacks, and showed her the emergency doors at the back of each room. When he started showing her how to oil the levers ("Just a *drop*, my dear!"), Property and Michael exchanged looks. They couldn't wait any longer, and they definitely didn't care about lever oil. So they backed away quietly and began to explore, the Gunther aboard Property's shoulder.

Michael's eyes were so wide that there was only just room for them on his face. Property knew how he felt. The Emporium was hard to take in.

On each door there was a lever, and by each lever there was a brass dial covered in tiny pictures. Michael had great trouble with the pictures and never knew what room he was calling up next. But they made perfect sense to Property. She pulled up room after room. A picture of a castle turret called up the Room of Knights and Castles, which had stone walls covered in tapestries and felt chilly. An airplane, obviously, brought the Room of Airplanes, which looked like a cockpit, with books making up the instrument panel.

The picture of a forest brought the Room of Woodland Tales, which had a pine needle floor and kept its books in trees, where there were actual living mice and birds. Something scurried past that might have been a vole. She had to shut that room quickly when the Gunther started purring too enthusiastically at a passing mouse.

Most of the pictures on the dial were obvious to Property, but some were strange. The picture of an old parchment, for example, was a mystery.

She turned the lever. The shop crunched especially wearily. It almost sounded as if fetching this room made the Emporium sad.

The room that arrived felt old. It smelled of vanilla. The light was dim, and the dust hung in the air in a respectful sort of way, as if it was sorry to disturb such an important room. Property ran a finger over the nearest books. All of them were beautiful and a bit broken.

"The Room of Old Books?" she asked the Gunther.

The kitten stuck his tongue out and dribbled.

"All right," she said, "the Room of Really, *Really* Old Books?"

Before the Gunther could comment, Montgomery came bobbing into the room, fluttering his hands. "My dear Property!" he said. "Whatever are you doing?"

"Um," said Property, who didn't think she was really *doing* anything.

"This is a terribly boring room," he said. "*Terribly* boring. You mustn't waste time in here. A load of old antiques. What's to see? What's to do? Come along, out we go, come along." And he shooed them outside.

Something had unsettled him. He took some hearty gulps of lemonade to steady himself, spilling a lot of it down his suit.

"Goodness me, look at the TIME!" he bellowed—which the Joneses helpfully tried to do, but as there didn't seem to be a clock on the shop floor, this was tricky. Montgomery began gabbling about trains that he had to catch and hunting for some papers that he needed, talking all the while. His ruddy face was far too ruddy, and his stretched-out smile was strained.

Property stood very still, watching him. She felt an urgent heartbeat, somewhere in her belly. It was six full years since she had been left behind in the White Hart, but she still knew perfectly well when somebody was abandoning something. What was Montgomery hiding?

The Gunther dug his claws into her shoulder particularly hard, as if to say that she should be paying more attention to him. Property tried to ignore him, but it was impossible to think while he needled her.

"What is it, you daft cat?" she whispered. And he looked at her as if there was something very important that he needed to say. He had folded one of his ears inside out, but other than that he was doing his best to look serious. Property was growing fond of him. He was so fierce for something so young.

Oh! He was *very* young. Which raised an interesting question.

Property whispered in the Gunther's ear. "Why did he buy you in the last month, little cat, if you can't go with him? Didn't he know he was going to leave?"

The Gunther preened himself smugly, like a cat who has made his point.

Montgomery had found his papers and was now hunting for a hat, muttering all the while. "Mr. Montgomery," said Property, trying to sound casual, "Where are you retiring to?"

"SPAIN!" exclaimed Montgomery.

The Joneses all looked at him. There is a limit to how loudly you need to say the word Spain. Albert H. Montgomery had exceeded that limit.

"Oh, lovely," said Netty brightly. "Whereabouts in Spain?"

"Florence."

"Florence," said Michael helpfully, "is in Italy."

Montgomery opened his mouth. Then he shut it again because this was true, and there was nothing more to be said. "Yes, quite, splendid," he said. "Now. The hour is here! The moment has come!" He had found his hat at last, and he rammed it onto his head and rammed a smile onto his face. "Well," he said, looking around the shop floor. "Well, well, well. I suppose this is goodbye."

His face reminded Property, with a sudden sharp pang, of her own feelings just a few hours earlier. "You know," she said kindly, "'Goodbye' just means 'God be with you.' That's all. It doesn't mean you can't come back."

Montgomery blinked at the staring girl with the funny name, who had managed to charm his monster-kitten into sitting on her shoulder like a parrot. Property didn't know it, but she could seem a bit strange at first. "Yes. Well. Splendid." He gave them all a little bow. "God be with you, then, my dear Joneses. And good luck."

And with that, Mr. Albert H. Montgomery himself took his coat from a hook behind the counter and walked out of the Great Montgomery Book Emporium without looking back.

That night, Michael and Property spent a long time choosing where to sleep. The Room of Bedtime Stories had a lot of beds they could use, but although they were excellent, squishy beds, the Joneses didn't like them: they didn't hug around you like a hammock. So they settled on the Room of Desert Islands, which had warm sand on the floor and potted palm trees to hang their hammocks from.

They set up their gas stove and kettle and had dinner, before reading a desert island adventure. Property quite liked the tough little hardback, but she *really* liked being in the room. She imagined that it felt a little like being able to read the book.

Then they strung their hammocks up on the potted palm trees for the night. Netty was the first to fall asleep. Property waited for her breathing to slow down and start doing that slight whistling on the in-breath, before she whispered, "Michael?"

"Mmm?"

"Why do you think Albert H. Montgomery gave this place up?"

He shrugged, joggling his hammock. "Old age?"

"He's not much older than Mum."

Michael thought about this. "New adventures?"

"ARGHOW!" said Property.

"You all right, Prop?"

Property fought the Gunther off her face and persuaded him to settle on her stomach instead. "Yes. I think this cat likes me."

"Rather you than me," said Michael, rolling over comfortably in his hammock.

"Don't you think it's odd, though? He could have sold this place for a lot of money."

Michael said something about running away from killer kittens that only half made sense, so Property knew that he was falling asleep. The Gunther was asleep too, it seemed. He was either snoring or he had swallowed a small drill.

Property wished that she was better at words. She couldn't quite name the worry that she felt, which made it hard to share and even harder to get rid of.

She was comforted by the darkness in the Emporium,

which was a deeper shade of black than the darkness at the White Hart and wrapped around her snugly. The Gunther was comforting too, warm on her belly. She shut her eyes and did her best to ignore the nameless worry, thinking instead about all the rooms that surrounded her—hundreds and hundreds of them, suspended in the darkness—just waiting to be called. It really was an Object of Wonder.

Rooms that she had seen that day started to get muddled up in her mind with rooms that only existed in her dreams, and her breathing started to slow. Little by little, breath by breath, Property Jones stopped paying attention for the day and drifted off to sleep.

All around her, the Emporium slept too, waiting for the morning.

Chapter Three

Eliot Pink

Property woke early to find the Gunther on her face and a wriggling deep in her belly. She wasn't sure whether the wriggling was excitement or worry, but whatever it was, it wouldn't let her go back to sleep. She moved the Gunther onto her shoulder, swung out of her hammock, and padded across the sand to the shop floor.

Two long windows set into the front door let in two slices of morning light, which turned the wood a rich honey color. There must have been traffic on the roads outside, but inside it was completely silent. The Emporium was still.

The stillness didn't last for long.

When they opened the doors at nine o'clock, there was already a line of customers outside. By ten o'clock, the shop was packed. Property had never realized that there were so many people in the world who wanted to buy books. It wasn't even raining.

She was by far the quickest of the Joneses at under-standing the picture-dials, so she soon found herself in charge of calling up the rooms. For those few happy hours, she forgot all about her secret: in *this* bookshop, she could find her way around better than anyone else.

While Property ran from room to room, Netty orga-nized the lines at each door, and Michael sat at the till. He was beaming so widely that he had trouble saying words properly and spent a lot of the morning saying, "Enjoy your beak!" to people, which puzzled them. (*You* try saying "book" while smiling. You'll see what I mean.)

Calling up the rooms was a lot of fun, but Property wished that there was time to linger in them. The most spectacular one to arrive that morning was the Room of Ocean Tales, which turned out to be a glass tank filled with fish of every color and eels and seahorses and crabs and even a billowing stingray. There was a tunnel through the middle that you could walk down, and the books were lying in wooden chests, like sunken treasure. She couldn't wait to show it to Michael that evening.

All morning the shop floor was filled with the chattering of customers and the grinding of rooms and the fluttering of hundreds of book pages. Everywhere Property turned, there was a confusion of movement and

sound. And that was why she noticed so *particularly* the man who arrived at noon: he was completely silent and completely still.

Apart from that, he wasn't remarkable. He was mostly made of a long, gray coat, with a long, gray face perched on top and shabby shoes underneath. He stood waiting in the middle of the shop, as if he expected someone to come and greet him. The crowd poured around him like a river around a stone.

A new room was needed, so Property turned away to help and never saw the man move. The next thing she knew he was at the counter, speaking to Michael. She paused to eavesdrop on her way across the shop.

"Hee can I help ye?" asked Michael. (He meant "How can I help you?" but you will remember the smiling difficulty).

"You can't," said the man. "Where's Montgomery?" His voice was deep and sounded like it had been put through a cheese grater.

Michael explained about Montgomery retiring to Florence in Spain, except that Florence isn't in Spain, so maybe he was in Italy, which is where Florence is. The man's face didn't change, but his fists made angry lumps in his coat pockets. Property had a feeling that he wasn't very interested in Spanish geography.

"I see," he said. "And who owns the shop now?"

"We do!" said Michael, practically singing. "We won it," he explained. "In a drawing," he added.

The man's left eyebrow rose a fraction. "I see," he said again. And then Netty started waving at Property to get a move on, and Property had to stop eavesdropping and get on with turning the rooms. She didn't get a moment's peace after that, but as she ran around the shop, she kept an eye on the counter. The man had a long conversation with Michael. Then he had a long conversation with Netty, who looked fiercely sensible. Michael wasn't smiling any more.

The Gunther bit Property's ear hard to get her attention, then spat in the man's direction, just in case Property hadn't realized that he was trouble.

"Ow! I'd already guessed," said Property. "Any more of that, and I'll put you back on the floor, ok?"

MAWR, said the Gunther. He licked his nose in shame.

The long conversation at the counter finally finished, and Netty came hurrying over. "Prop, love," she said, "could you tell the customers that they've got five more minutes, and then we need to close the shop?"

"Why?"

"Nothing to worry about. I'll explain in a minute," replied Netty, and she hurried away again to start shooing customers out. Property was not reassured. "Nothing to worry about" was what Netty had said when she found a five-year-old girl in her lost property cupboard. From Netty, "Nothing to worry about" could mean anything from a sneeze to the total collapse of space and time. But there was nothing to do except wait patiently for five minutes to find out more.

Of course, people didn't leave within five minutes because people are famously a nuisance. The Gunther helped by nibbling at people's heels if they were too slow, but it was still half an hour before the last customer had been rounded up and sent away. One woman locked herself in the Room of Prison Stories and had to be lured out of her cell with free-book vouchers. At last, the shop floor was empty, apart from the Joneses and the long, gray man. Netty shut the front door.

"What's going on?" said Property.

"Property," said Netty, "this is Mr. Eliot Pink."

"Hello," said Property. If Eliot Pink heard her, he didn't let it show.

Netty carried on. "He sold the Emporium a special

book, and he hasn't been paid yet. Montgomery was going to sell it on to a customer first, you see, and it seems he never did."

Everyone was looking very serious. Property was puzzled. How bad could it be? Books didn't cost all that much.

"Was it an expensive book?" she asked.

Netty looked helplessly at Michael.

"It's the script for a Shakespeare play," Michael explained, wide-eyed. "Handwritten by *Shakespeare himself*. It's a new discovery. It's the only one in the whole world that is actually in his handwriting."

Property didn't know much about Shakespeare, except that he had a shelf to himself at the White Hart, and people always said his name in a special hushed voice. "Is that a big deal, then?" she asked.

Eliot's left eyebrow rose slightly, and he spoke at last. "Quite a big deal, yes. I sold it to Montgomery for forty-three million pounds."

Property gaped at him. That was an incredible amount of money. "Forty-thr— but...we don't have anything like forty-three million pounds," she said.

"So I gather," said Eliot.

"It's all simple, and fine, and simply fine," said Netty—

although she didn't sound convinced. "We just need to find the play. That's all." And she looked around at the dozen doors of the Emporium, each one with hundreds of rooms behind it.

Property remembered a room full of yellowing books and dust and the smell of vanilla. She remembered Montgomery shooing her out of there. She thought two things at once, but she only said one of them out loud.

What she *said* was, "I know which room it's in."

And what she thought was, *but I have a feeling that this isn't going to be that easy.*

The others were hugely relieved. "Oh well *done*, Property," said Netty. "That's wonderful. Wonderful! You lead the way then, love!" She turned to Eliot. "Do have a seat, Mr. Pink, and we'll be back in a moment. Help yourself to something to read."

But Eliot stayed standing. Property led the Joneses to the Room of Old Books. The Gunther stayed behind on the counter to guard Eliot, lying on his back with his legs in the air and glaring at him upside down.

There was an almighty groaning and sighing from the Emporium when Property called the room, and it took much too long to come. At last, it arrived with a sorry wheeze. The three of them stepped inside.

"Right," said Netty, "One wall each." And she started scanning the left-hand wall.

Michael took the back wall. With a familiar flush of panic, Property turned to her right. Her secret was being a nuisance again. How would she know an old Shakespeare play when she found one?

Pushing down the panic, she picked up the nearest book and began to search for clues. It was a creaking, fat book bound in broken leather, and it felt *very* important. The words picked out in gold on the spine looked long and difficult. When she opened it, it sighed enormously, and a pile of loose pages and dust came tumbling out onto the floor.

She picked one of the pages up and examined it. It was a worn yellow-y brown. It was not any sort of paper that she was used to: it was thicker and rougher.

The room was dim, so she held the sheet up to one of the lamps to get a better look. There were straight lines running across it, faint marks that glowed in the light. Was that any sort of clue?

"Michael," she said, "what are the lines on the paper?"

Michael didn't look up from sorting papers at lightning speed. "If it's handmade paper, there'll be marks from the frame mold that was used to make it. We didn't start using machines to make paper until the 1800s."

"Oh." Property was pretty sure that Shakespeare died ages before then, so this was a start: she was looking for handmade paper. But that was most of the room, by the looks of it, so she would need something else. "Why does it smell of vanilla?"

"There used to be a thing called lignin in paper. It smells like that when it gets old."

"Oh." Property tried out the word *lignin* in her head. It was a lovely, singsong word. But it didn't really help.

She tried a different line of thought. If it was so valuable, it wouldn't just be lying around on one of these careless piles. And Montgomery hadn't wanted her to find it, so he would surely have hidden it away somewhere.

There were some cupboards along the bottom of the wall. Most had keys in the locks: old-fashioned iron keys with twisted heads. She opened them one by one, but they were full of huge leather books—much too big to be a single play.

The last cupboard didn't have a key. Happily, locks were as easy for Property as the mechanical bookshop had been: they were just a matter of paying *attention*.

She pulled a hairpin from her head, eased it in, and felt for the telltale grooves of the lock. With a little work, it swung open.

The thing inside was not a leather book. Property wasn't sure what it was.

She took it out. It was the same yellow-brown shade as all the other old paper, but it was blotchy, as if something had been spilled on it. A couple of pages fluttered from the top, tattered and torn, covered in a mess of smeared ink. It looked as though someone had tried, unsuccessfully, to peel these pages away from the rest, which were stuck together. This stickiness was puzzling. It didn't smell of glue. Or of vanilla, for that matter. Instead, it smelled like lemons and sugar, with a sickly scent that reminded Property of licorice.

She looked in the cupboard again. The only other item was a bottle. She took it out. It was an almost-empty bottle of lemonade.

"Mum," she said.

"Yes?"

"I think"—and Property looked at the useless, ruined pages in her hand and took a deep breath—"Mum, I think Albert H. Montgomery might have spilled a bottle of lemonade all over his important play."

Netty and Michael turned to look. For a long time none of them said anything.

"This is definitely it," said Michael, looking at one of the loose sheets. "You can make out the first bit of 'Shakespeare,' if you squint at it a bit." His squint made him look startlingly like the Gunther. "Well," he said, when no one else spoke, "this explains a lot. Montgomery couldn't possibly sell this. He's run off because he can't pay that horrible man, and he's left us to clean up the mess."

"Could it still be worth something?" said Property.

"No," said Netty. "Not nearly enough to cover the debt, anyway." And her mouth twitched a few times as if she was trying to find something else to say—something sensible and kind—but nothing came out.

"So...so what happens?" Property asked.

"Well, Eliot said if we can't pay, he'll take whatever we have," said Netty in a very small voice. "The Emporium, of course—and our savings—and the White Hart."

Michael banged his fist on one of the tables, sending up a cloud of dust. "Ow," he said (because he'd overdone the banging), and then, "I *hate* Albert H. Montgomery! He should be the one paying Eliot. How could he just run off like that?"

No one had an answer to that. It was a cowardly

thing to do. But Property found that she felt a bit sorry for Montgomery. A once-in-a-lifetime opportunity, and he went and spilled lemonade all over it. Property had to admit that *she* wouldn't fancy sticking around to explain that to Eliot Pink either.

They trooped back to the shop floor, where he was waiting. There were now another six men with him, all with droopy faces and wispy mustaches. They looked like unhappy walruses that had accidentally put on overalls.

"These are the Wollup brothers," said Eliot. "They work for me. They'll be clearing the shop, if you can't pay." He looked at the Joneses one by one. "And, judging by your faces, I'm guessing that you can't?"

Netty explained the situation. Eliot's eyebrows twitched at the part about the lemonade, but he didn't get upset. Instead he just shrugged, gave some instructions to the Wollups, then turned back to Netty. "We need to discuss what else you own. That cat looks valuable, for a start. I will have my partner, Mr. Gimble, draw up the paperwork, and we can sign in the morning. You can stay until then, but get ready to leave first thing tomorrow."

And with that, Eliot steered Netty to the counter, while five Wollups lumbered toward five doors, clutching

boxes. The sixth picked up a crate and looked uncertainly at the Gunther. The kitten bared his teeth.

"I can't watch this," said Michael, and he went to sit with the dictionaries for a while.

Property couldn't blame him. It was horrible to see the Emporium being torn apart. Within a few short hours, the first dozen rooms were just empty, gaping holes. Boxes of books filled the shop floor, lamps lay in piles, and one crate was stuffed full of unhappy woodland creatures. The only comfort was that, so far, the Gunther had escaped capture (the sixth Wollup had taken a break to weep nervously in an armchair).

The whole time that the Emporium was being taken apart, Eliot Pink stood in the middle of it all, still and silent and gray, like a shadow that has come unstuck from someone's heels.

"If I were you," Property said to him, "I'd have kept it as a bookshop. It was much nicer." But he curled his fists up in his pockets again and didn't answer. So Property went to join Michael in the Room of Dictionaries instead.

She sat next to him, and he put his arm around her. "All right, Prop?"

"Not really. I wish we'd never left the White Hart."

Michael sighed. "Me too."

"What are we going to do, Michael? Where are we going to live?"

Michael looked helplessly down at the dictionary in his lap, as if it might have the answer. But this was not that sort of question, so he was forced to say something that Property had never heard him say in her whole life. Three small words that sounded wrong in Michael's voice: "I don't know."

Chapter Four

Property Pays Attention

That night, Property couldn't sleep. For the first time that she could remember, the Joneses hadn't read together that evening. Netty had gone to her hammock early without saying a word, and Michael had said that he didn't really feel like reading that evening and got into his own hammock soon after. Now they were both breathing deeply. Only Property was awake.

The Wollups stayed the night. They had tried to use the Room of Bedtime Stories, but as soon as they lay down, the air-conditioning in there had turned itself on to its coldest setting and refused to be turned off. Now they were dozing under their coats on the shop floor, snoring enormously. Eliot stayed too. If he was asleep—and it was difficult to tell—then he had fallen asleep standing up.

At last Property gave up and tipped herself out of her hammock. She tiptoed out to find a book to look at. It was too strange to try and sleep without the ritual page-turning.

Three doors were open on the shop floor: the Room of Dictionaries; the Room of Sticky Endings, which had got stuck and wouldn't budge no matter how hard the Wollups tried; and the Room of Old Books. Property didn't really want to think about that last room. She took a dictionary in honor of Michael, chose an armchair as far from Eliot and the Wollups as possible, turned on a lamp, and began to turn the thin, whispering pages.

It smelled strongly of Michael's favorite shelf at the White Hart. She held it close to her face and breathed in. As she so often did, she wondered what it was like to really *read* those mysterious markings.

A shadow twitched at the edge of the lamplight.

"Has anyone ever told you," it said, "what a strange little girl you are?" And Eliot Pink came near enough to the lamp to be slightly more than a shadow. He stayed just outside the puddle of light.

Property told herself that it was only the half-light that made him look sinister. Still, she couldn't help wondering whether the others, asleep in the Room of Desert Islands, would hear her if she yelled.

"You stare too much," said Eliot. "And you blink less than other people."

Property considered this. "You move less than other people," she said. "Especially your face."

To her amazement, Eliot laughed—a single *ha*. "True. You're observant. Is your name really Property?"

Property nodded.

"Well then, Miss Property Jones. A word of advice. You can't eat books."

"I know that."

"Well, you looked like you were trying."

"I was just smelling it," said Property defensively. There was a short silence, which seemed to suggest that maybe smelling books wasn't *entirely* normal either.

"Funny way to read, wouldn't you say?" said Eliot.

Property's stomach backflipped. Surely he couldn't have guessed? She blathered, panicked. "I just think it's interesting, that's all. They all smell different. Like, the old books, they smell of lignin. Although not the play, obviously—that just smells of sugar and lemon now, and something I couldn't place. It was...a bit licorice-y. And really new books smell fresh, but it depends how good the paper is, and..." Property had a feeling that she was making things worse. She thought she saw Eliot's face twitch an especially violent twitch, but the shadows were shifting confusingly, and it was hard to be sure. "The words are good too," she added lamely.

He raised his eyebrows, then changed the subject without warning. "You don't look like the other two," he said. "You're blonder and taller, and your hair isn't as curly. They're not your real family, are they?"

"They *are*. They found me in a cupboard."

"That's a no, then," said Eliot. "I'm surprised they put up with you. What use is an illiterate kid in a bookshop?"

Property considered this. "What's *illiterate*?"

A muscle near Eliot's mouth wriggled into an almost-smirk. "A word you ought to know. Means you can't read."

Property felt sick. So he *did* know.

"It *almost* seems," he continued, "as if the others don't know about it. But I'm sure that can't be right. After all, you say they are *family*. It was obvious to me as soon as you picked up a book."

"They *are* family." Property's eyes stung. "They just don't always pay attention."

"Probably a wise idea not to mention it now, though, if they don't already know. I'm sure they'd be pretty hurt that you've lied to them all this time."

Property wanted to scream at him to stop talking, but all she said was, "Why did you come over here?"

"Why did *you*?" Eliot took a pace forwards, and he was lit up for a moment. He paused a long, gray pause. Then he seemed to change his mind about something. He pointed to the Room of Desert Islands. "Time you were in bed, Property Jones."

He spat out her name like a bad word. Property had no idea what she had done to make him so angry. Part of her wanted to refuse to leave, just to be stubborn, but a larger part of her wanted to get away from him as quickly as she could. The larger part won. She got up from the chair and crossed the shop floor, while Eliot Pink followed.

It felt as if he had cast some strange spell with his cruelty, and Property couldn't think straight. The spell was broken by the Gunther, who dropped on them with a great war cry from above. He seemed to be aiming for Eliot's shoulder, but missed, and ended up scrabbling madly for a hold on his coat.

There was a lot of paw-flailing from the cat and a lot of muttering from Eliot. The Gunther managed to hang on by his claws to Eliot's pocket. Eliot tugged him off, but ripped the pocket down the seam in the process, sending loose change and tissues and sweets rolling across the floor. The Gunther flew after them with an unhappy *MAWR* as Eliot flung him aside.

"I've changed my mind about the cat," said Eliot. "You can keep it. Go to bed." And he marched three paces away, back to where he had been standing before, and shut his eyes.

Property scooped up the Gunther and went back to her hammock. She climbed into it obediently. But inside, she wasn't feeling obedient, and she wasn't planning to sleep. Something had set her heart pounding, and the something was this:

The sweets in Eliot's pocket had been licorice.

She had swept up one of the licorice sticks while she was picking up the Gunther. Eliot hadn't seemed to notice. She clutched it in her hand now and remembered the violent twitch of his face at the mention of the little sweet. What did it mean?

She wasn't sure, but she had to try to find out.

She waited half an hour, to give Eliot time to fall asleep. Then another five minutes, to be sure. Then another one minute, for luck.

The Gunther climbed onto her face and looked into her left eye very sternly.

"I know," whispered Property. "And I *will* go, but how do I know if he's asleep?"

The Gunther leapt off her face and padded out into the entrance hall. As quietly as she could, Property dropped out of the hammock and crept across the sand to watch. In the dark, everyone was a silhouette, but she could just about make out the shadow of the Gunther crossing over to the shadow of Eliot and nosing him gently. Then a little less gently. Nothing.

The little cat jerked his head at Property, and she followed him out and crossed the shop floor.

Even when they were among the lignin and dust with the door shut, Property didn't dare turn on one of the tall lamps. Instead she used a small desk lamp that let out the softest of light. To be on the safe side, she stacked up some papers in front of it to dull the light even more. The marks from the frame mold glowed in the lamplight. She kneeled by the lamp with the play and took a good look at the licorice stick.

"What am I looking for, cat?" she whispered.

The Gunther looked as helpful as he could, turning his ears inside out and opening his eyes very wide, but that didn't answer the question. Property's heart slowed down a little. For a glorious moment, she had felt so sure that she was onto something important. But now that she was here, she had no idea what she was looking for.

She unwrapped the licorice—a black stick in a clear cellophane wrapper. It stank. She hated licorice. She held it in her palm and realized that she was sweating; the licorice left a sticky mess.

"Ugh," she whispered, "I don't know why anyone eats this stuff, cat." And she wiped her hand on her pajama trousers. This turned out to be a really bad idea. Moist licorice leaves a smear the color of poo. It *almost* seemed to Property as if the Gunther was laughing at her.

"All right, I know what it looks like. But now is not the time," she scolded him. She turned to the play.

Then she looked at her trousers.

Then she looked at the play.

"Cat," she breathed, "can you turn paper brown with licorice?" Michael had shown her once how to make paper look old with wet teabags. They soaked pages in the pale brown liquid and left them out to dry. Did wet licorice do the same?

She took the least-important-looking paper from a stack of nearby old letters, sucked the end of the licorice, and dragged it across the paper. It was a dark brown, too dark. Maybe she needed some water?

There wasn't any nearby; she would have to improvise. She scrambled over to the cupboard where she had found the play, and took out Montgomery's lemonade. There was still about an inch of liquid left in there. She put the licorice in it, counted to thirty seconds (although to be honest she raced through the last ten seconds *very* quickly), then poured a bit of the licorice-liquid on her finger and dragged it over the page.

The paper turned a nasty yellow-brown.

"Is the play a fake?" she whispered to the Gunther. He squished his face up in delight. "Is that a yes? Oh—wait, I know how to check!"—and she shoved the papers in front of the lamp aside, and held one of the loose leaves of the play up to the light. There were no lines from the mold. The paper was ripped and torn, but perfectly smooth. She tried another. They were all the same.

The paper was machine-made.

"Modern paper! Michael said we didn't use machines until the 1800s, cat. Shakespeare has been dead for...oh I don't know, years and years and years. He can't have written this." Property was so happy that she did a foolish thing. She kissed the Gunther on the top of his head. The Gunther hissed and attacked her nose. It bled a bit, but Property didn't care. She had to tell the others. It was a fake! They didn't owe any money at all!

She flung open the door and came nose to long, gray nose with Eliot Pink.

"You," he said, "are a deceitful little girl."

Property worked extra-hard at not blinking, just to annoy him. "*You* sold Montgomery a fake play and tried to cheat us out of forty-three million pounds. It doesn't have any mold marks." She held up the sticky piece of licorice. "You dropped this, by the way."

Eliot did not take the licorice. There was a nasty silence.

"I see," he said.

He thought a long, gray thought.

"I think," he said, "on balance, that it would be better if you didn't mention that to anyone else until tomorrow. We can have a little chat about it *after* your mother has signed my papers."

And before Property could disagree, Eliot had shut the door. There was a sudden crunch, and the whole room lurched. Property only had time to think "What on earth...?" before the room lurched again, and she fell back against a bookcase. She felt her head meet the wood. Then everything went dark.

Chapter Five

In the Stacks

When Property woke she was still in the Room of Old Books, only now a headache was there with her. This was, she decided, a setback. She lay groaning on the floor for a minute, until it occurred to her how much more pleasant it would be to lie groaning in a hammock. So with a great effort, she got up to open the door to the shop floor.

The only problem was the shop floor wasn't there anymore. Where the door should have been, there was just a stone wall.

Property took a few deep breaths. She wondered if this could be an illusion caused by the headache, decided that this was unlikely, and tried to think something more useful. Through the pulsing of the headache, a sensible thought reached her brain, and she realized what was going on.

Eliot had switched the rooms. He had put her in the stacks.

Then she remembered *why* he had put her in the stacks and became dimly aware that she ought to be getting an urgent message to Netty. She waited for another sensible thought to arrive, but nothing came, so she just thought *Help* and *Oh*. The Gunther padded over and bit her ankles in an encouraging fashion. She stooped down to pet him.

"This isn't good," she said, "is it, cat?"

MAWR said the Gunther. He sounded a little less aggressive than usual.

"So what do we do?"

The Gunther put his head on one side and swished his tail thoughtfully, eyes shut. For a minute Property thought he had gone to sleep. Then he got up, spat at a passing piece of dust, and butted his head at a smaller door on the other side of the room. It was the emergency door that Montgomery had shown Netty. Property followed and opened it.

She looked out, and her stomach turned itself inside-out like one of the Gunther's ears. She withdrew hastily.

"Bad plan," she said. But then, the more she thought about it, the more she couldn't think of any other plans. She peered back out again.

They were facing an open space with a sickening drop. The floor was out of sight. Above and below, stretching as far as Property could see, there were more rooms, suspended by a complicated system of ropes and chains. If she stuck her head out far enough to the left and right, she could see the next stacks on either side. The whole place was cold and silent, hanging like bones in a skeleton.

She withdrew again to give her stomach some time to right itself. What with her inside-out stomach and her pounding head, she was very tempted to curl up in that nice cupboard where she had found the play and have a nap.

But the longer she sat, the more she remembered. The word *illiterate* wandered into her head and eventually found words like *use* and *bookshop* that seemed to belong with it. Rearranged, they said:

Use a kid in what bookshop is an illiterate

which didn't make sense, so she tried again and made:

What use is an illiterate kid in a bookshop?

Then she regretted trying to remember anything.

"I'm *not* useless," she told the Gunther. "I'm the only one who spotted that the play's a fake." But even as she said it, she realized that this wasn't much use at all out here in the stacks. She had to tell the others before they signed Eliot's papers, or else she was every bit as useless as he had said.

She spoke sternly to her stomach about the importance of staying the right way up and opened the door once again. The darkness below felt so huge, she half-believed it could reach into the room and pull her out. She tried not to look.

The Gunther came to join her and promptly fell over the edge.

"No!" gasped Property, leaning forward without thinking and almost toppling after.

There was a proud *MAWR* from just below. The Gunther was hanging from the thickest of the ropes, perfectly content. He climbed up and down the rope a little, as if to show how easy it was.

"That," said Property, "is mad."

But then, the situation was urgent. The Joneses were about to lose everything they had. And now she was remembering an icy voice saying, *They'd be pretty hurt that you've lied to them all this time*, and she was determined to do something so good that no one could ever doubt her loyalty to her family, even for a second. Climbing the ropes might be mad, but it was *possible*, and that was a start.

She'd need to find a room that was currently on the shop floor. Michael had definitely opened the Room of Dictionaries, one door to the right of the Room of Old Books. If she could cross over to that stack, maybe she could find it.

But how could she get across?

An uncomfortably long way below, there was a metal bar running between the stacks. She could probably get over that way, if she climbed down to it on the rope. Even then, it would be a long job to find the right door.

MAWR, said the Gunther impatiently.

"All right, all right. Little beast," said Property. And she leaned out to the side and gripped the rope firmly. Then, with a deep breath, she swung out of the Room of Old Books and put her whole weight on the rope.

All the rooms on the stack rattled at this unexpected disturbance. Property's stomach quit the whole situation and went to live a quiet life at the top of her throat.

The stacks were cold and cavernous. Property instantly regretted her decision, but before she could change her mind, she lost her grip and slithered down several feet of rope. She let out a scream, and it echoed around the stacks long after she had finished. It sounded as though the Emporium itself was screaming.

For a minute after that she stayed very still, clutching at the rope with her eyes tightly shut.

This was a terrible idea; she had to get back inside. When she could bear to open her eyes again, she began to inch down toward the closest room, one careful hand at a time.

Moving down the rope, she began to feel a little less scared. It wasn't so difficult, once she got into the rhythm of climbing—as long as she didn't think about the drop. She began to climb a little faster, and when she reached the next door, she hesitated. Now that she had come this far, perhaps it wasn't such a bad idea to keep going?

The Gunther *MAWR*ed from somewhere below her feet. Property made up her mind. "Coming!" she called, which echoed in a determined sort of way—*Coming! Coming! Coming!* And she ignored the welcoming door and carried on down the rope.

The climb down made her arms ache and tremble. When she reached the strip of metal, it was not as wide as she had hoped, and the floor was still so far away that it was out of sight. The Gunther struck out merrily enough, but that is all very well if you are a cat and have nine lives. As far as Property was aware, she only had one life. And until strangers had started turning it all upside down, it had been a life that she was fond of.

She put one foot on the bar. She would have preferred to crawl across it instead of walking, but it wasn't quite wide enough. Getting off the rope was the worst of it; once she was there, she could put out both arms for balance. The metal was cold against her bare feet.

She walked across very, very carefully. The stacks seemed to hold their breath.

Climbing back off again at the other side, the coarse feel of rope between her palms and soles felt like heaven.

"Up or down?" she asked the cat, who hung below her. He shrugged, wobbling.

Every instinct in Property shouted at her to get closer to the ground, so she carried on downwards. At each room, she took one arm off the rope and bashed open the door, glimpsing the room inside before it banged shut again.

It was strange to see the rooms from back here, warm and inviting, like scenes from another world. Pirate ship and boarding school, dragon's cave and snowy tundra, painted caravan and giant bird's nest, all flashed in and

out of view. A theater and a tea party and a junkyard and a circus tent. And suddenly, there!—the Room of Dictionaries!

"*Yes!*" cried Property. She swung hard against the rope to prepare for her final leap. The whole stack rattled, as if in applause.

All that remained was to get back inside. With one final swing, she gave the door a hearty kick and let go of the rope. The door swung inwards, and she went flying in after it, letting it bang shut behind her.

The Room of Dictionaries was waiting patiently, ever so clean and bright and polite. Property gave a small sob of relief. For a few lovely seconds she just lay there in the light, checking that she still had all the body parts that she had started out with. Her stomach slipped back to its rightful place and tried to pretend that it had been on board with the plan the whole time.

MAWR, said an angry voice.

"Oh, sorry," said Property. And she opened the door to let the Gunther in too.

With the kitten restored to her shoulder, Property turned to the open door facing the shop floor. It was already light out there, and she could hear movement and voices. She realized that she had no idea how long she had been unconscious—or any real concept of how long she had spent climbing the stacks. It was already morning.

Surely she wasn't too late?

Chapter Six

Outside

It took Property a moment to adjust to being back on the shop floor. In the weak morning sunlight, it looked dreary and defeated. Boxes littered the floor, Wollups were yawning in armchairs, and the piles of books looked lifeless and dull. Every movement echoed.

Netty was up, but not Michael, so Property guessed that it was sometime between eight and nine. She was always up and out of her hammock long before the others, so Netty probably hadn't even noticed she was missing.

Netty looked tea-deprived and befuddled. Next to her, Eliot was folding away some papers. The corners of his mouth almost looked as though they might be smiling.

"STOP!" Property yelled.

Netty and the half-awake Wollups looked at Property in confusion. It wasn't clear what they were meant to be stopping. One of the Wollups sat entirely still to be on the safe side.

MAWR, explained the Gunther.

This didn't help.

"Don't sign anything," Property said, picking her way across the shop floor.

Eliot raised one eyebrow a fraction.

"How did you get out?"

"I climbed."

"Climbed what?" said Netty.

"The stacks," said Property. "Listen, the important thing is—"

"Why were you in the *stacks*?"

"I put her there," explained Eliot.

"WHAT?"

"Look," said Property, "I'll explain later, the important thing is—"

"Good morning," said Michael, shuffling out of the Room of Desert Islands and shaking a pile of sand out of his hair.

"Michael," said Netty, "*please* shake the sand out in the desert, not the shop floor."

"I *did*," said Michael, folding his arms and dislodging more sand.

"MUM," said Property, "listen. Don't sign anything. We don't owe any money. The play's a fake."

Netty's mouth had already started to tell Michael off about the sand. It changed its mind and hovered around an O-shape for a while in confusion. At last, she said, "Oh." She didn't sound as pleased as Property had hoped.

"You're too late," said Eliot. "Mr. Gimble brought the papers round twenty minutes ago. We've signed."

"But if we don't owe you anything—" Netty began.

"Then you have very kindly given me two bookshops," he finished, "and all your money. As a gift." He smirked. "How thoughtful of you."

"That," said Property, "is *cheating.*"

"Gosh," said Eliot, "so it is."

"Um," said Michael, "I'm a bit confused."

"Delightful as this little chat is," said Eliot, "I'd prefer it if you didn't have it on my property. Time to go." And he opened the door and waited.

"No," said Netty.

Eliot raised one eyebrow. "Pardon?"

"This isn't right," said Netty. She was doing her firmest voice, the one that made Michael and Property do whatever she said *at once.* "We've been tricked. I want my signature back. You can't expect to walk in here and take everything from my family and get away with it."

"I rather think I can," said Eliot. And he signaled to three Wollups, who took hold of a Jones each. Property squirmed against the Wollup's heavy hand, which did no good. The Gunther launched a heroic defense, but the other three Wollups got up to restrain him too, and after that he could only *MAWR* and spit.

"I don't know why you're so shocked," said Eliot, talking over Netty, who was still arguing. "It's your own fault. You should have wondered why you were being given a free bookshop. And that fool Montgomery should have checked the play properly. If you people can't be bothered to pay attention, then someone smarter than you will cheat you, in the end." He turned away from them and waved a hand. "Get them out."

And the Wollups pushed them outside, ignoring Netty's sensible arguments and Michael's clever thoughts about justice and the Gunther's spitting. The door was shut on the Joneses with a heavy bang. For a minute, they carried on yelling and hammering at the door, until at last it sank in that nobody was listening.

Out here on the pavement, the world carried on as if nothing had happened. People ambled past. A driver

honked his horn. The dull November light made London look a bit peaky, and everything shivered in the wind, including the Joneses.

Property looked at her mother and brother, hoping that one of them was going to know what to do now. Neither of them spoke. Michael was blinking very fast.

"Michael," said Property, "what happened to your glasses?" There was a thin crack all the way across one of the lenses.

"The Gunther," said Michael, "I think he was trying to help, but he missed." The Gunther *MAWR*ed sheepishly at their ankles.

Netty made a noise that was either a laugh or a sob. "That cat," she said, "is a nightmare. Come here, you two." And she hugged them both and took a couple of long, shaky breaths. "Well," she said, still holding on to them tightly, "we can't stand here worrying all day, eh? Let's find somewhere to sit down and have a think." She ruffled Property's hair. "And I need to hear what you've been up to, Prop. Sounds like you've had quite the adventure."

Netty was pretending to be all right, but her voice was a little *too* bright. Property wished that she was better with words and could say something kind. But she couldn't think of anything, so she just nodded.

They looked up and down the street. There was a fancy-looking café across the road called the Café Splendide, but after counting the change in her pocket, Netty decided that it might be wise to just sit in the bus shelter. They perched on the red plastic seat, a little squashed.

Property explained everything that had happened, leaving out the bit about being illiterate and useless. When she told them about the stacks, Michael let out a bellow of rage. A nervous young man, who had been waiting for a bus, quickly decided that it was a nice day for a walk and hurried away.

"Property Jones," said Netty, when she had finished, "you are *brilliant.*"

"But I was too late." Property didn't feel brilliant. If only she hadn't spent so long feeling sorry for herself. Things could have been so different.

The Gunther climbed comfortingly onto her head, but nobody knew what to say. The wind rushed past them, making them all shiver, breezing off to wherever it was going. But where should the Joneses go?

"Well," said Netty, "I suppose the first thing to do is to complain to the police."

No one thought that this was likely to do very much

good, but they agreed to try. Which was all very well, but they no longer had a telephone, and none of them knew where the nearest police station was.

Netty asked passersby, and eventually someone told them to take the number six bus. It turned out that Netty didn't have enough change for all of them to get on the bus, so she went alone, and the other two waited for her at the bus stop.

"Look after your sister, Michael," she said, as she stepped on board. And Michael nodded solemnly, as if this was very reasonable. As if Property hadn't just spent the night proving that she was more than capable of looking after herself.

Property didn't mind. Michael could take charge for a bit if he wanted to. She was suddenly *very* tired.

Michael did his looking-at-her-properly thing. "Prop, did you sleep at all?" She shook her head, and he put his arm round her and said, "Have a nap." And that was the most sensible thing that Property had heard since they left the White Hart. So she did.

It was a fitful doze, interrupted over and over again by the wind, and full of dreams. She dreamed about ropes and rattling doors and the smell of vanilla in dark rooms. She dreamed that she was trying to tell Netty something urgent, but there was an ocean full of Wollup-walruses in the way. She dreamed that she was alone at the bus stop because Michael had found out that she had lied about being able to read and had left in a huff.

When a man in plum-colored velvet started warbling, Property thought that he was a dream too. But then Michael replied, and she could feel his voice rumbling in his chest—not like a dream-voice at all. So she dragged herself into wakefulness.

There, entirely real, was Albert H. Montgomery himself.

Michael and Montgomery were having an argument. Michael was getting more and more spluttery, and his glasses were getting further and further down his nose, while Montgomery kept trying to say something about breakfast. It seemed to Property that breakfast was a colossally important idea. She wished Michael would stop interrupting him.

"I'd like breakfast," she announced.

The argument stopped, as both of them turned to look at her. The Gunther purred approvingly.

"Well, there we go then," said Montgomery. "Splendid."

Michael opened his mouth to argue, looked at his shivering sister, and shut it again. Property felt him taking some deep breaths, like he did whenever a customer was rude about a favorite book. "Fine," he said. And they stood up and followed Montgomery into the Café Splendide.

It turned out to be a very fancy café indeed. It was all decked out in pink and gold, with huge bunches of lilies in crystal vases and chandeliers hanging from the ceiling. It was all a bit much. Property was still only half-awake, and it was thoroughly muddling to be in a glitzy café when just a short time ago she had been climbing around in the stacks. *And,* her brain sleepily protested, *what is Albert H. Montgomery himself doing here, anyway?*

The waiter at the door didn't look too sure about the teenage boy in too-small clothes or the little girl with a goblin-cat on her head. But he was *very* sure about Montgomery, who was clearly a regular. He ushered them to the best table. With amazing speed, more waiters appeared with three jugs of lemonade.

"Splendid, thank you," said Montgomery. "And I will have the knickerbocker glory breakfast special, please."

"Very good, Monsieur Montgomery," said the waiter. "And for the young Monsieur and Mademoiselle?"

Property ordered a hot breakfast, because her night-time adventures had left her starving. Michael ordered a hot breakfast too because you never really need an excuse. Their orders arrived double-quick. Michael was still trying to look angry, but it is very hard to look angry at a delicious hot breakfast.

"Mr. Montgomery," said Property, "why have you come back?"

Montgomery blew some sad bubbles in his lemonade through his straw while he considered how to reply. "I was hoping," he said, "to put things right. *I* should have been the one to lose everything to Pink. I was coming back to face him myself. But young Michael informs me that I was too late."

Property had been half-asleep at the time, but she was pretty sure that young Michael had been a lot less polite than that.

"I owe you an apology, my dear Joneses. And an explanation, perhaps. Not that it will excuse what I did." He produced a photo from his jacket pocket. It showed five children and a rather stern woman, all dressed in plum-colored velvet. "This is my family," he said. "My wife, Aramanthea, is a good woman. Very good. Yes. A much finer woman than I deserve." He had an encouraging nibble of ice cream. "I rather disappoint her, I'm afraid. She doesn't approve of all the lemonade I drink. Seems to think I have rather a problem."

He paused hopefully, so Property said, "Oh, really?

Surely not." Michael had a mouth full of hash browns and couldn't talk, so he just looked surprised. The Gunther had a mouth full of Property's hash brown and didn't care a fig what Montgomery was talking about.

Montgomery sighed. "I never told her about the play. All our money, lost! I *couldn't*. She would have left me, I'm sure, and taken the children too. She is always saying I'm a bad influence on them." He looked sadly at the photo. "Such a *very* good woman."

The Joneses didn't know what to say. They looked at their plates. The Gunther discovered baked beans, which he had never eaten before, and he started purring furiously.

"I have always believed," Montgomery continued, "that I would do anything for my splendid children. But when I met you, my dear Joneses, it was all rather more difficult than I expected. To be frank, you were off-puttingly *nice*. I found I couldn't cheat you after all. I had to try and undo the damage." He raised his eyebrows at Property. "You were quite right, Miss Jones—most unfortunately, saying goodbye didn't mean I couldn't come back."

The waiter came gliding over to check on the food.

"Is everything to your satisfaction, Monsieur?"

"Not really," said Montgomery, staring into his lemonade. "I believe I may be a terrible sham of a human being."

The waiter bobbed a small bow and went gliding off very fast like a startled duck.

Montgomery sighed. "Can you forgive me?"

Property found, to her surprise, that she could. She didn't even have to try very hard. He *had* tried to put it right, after all. And she knew all about doing stupid things for your family.

Michael was harder to please. He folded his arms. "Do you realize we have nowhere to live?"

"My dear Michael," said Montgomery, "I promise you that I will make sure you have everything you need."

This should have been a relief. Instead, Property suddenly felt choked up, because all she needed in the world at that moment was the lost property cupboard in the White Hart, and Eliot had that now. "It's not fair," she said. "He's cheating, and I caught him, and we should have won. I just want to go home."

Montgomery didn't know what she was talking about, so Michael filled him in on the whole licorice business, while Property stroked the Gunther and tried to feel a bit less lost. As Michael talked, Montgomery got redder and redder and redder.

"The rascal!" he exclaimed, when Michael had finished. "I can't believe it! *Ahforjeree!*"

"Bless you," said Property. But Michael explained that a *forgery* was just another word for a fake, and that it comes from the old French word *forgier*, which meant "to shape something metal over a fire." Before Property could ask what fire had to do with anything, Montgomery was off again.

"The scoundrel! The thief! The knave!" he bellowed. "This cannot be allowed. I will *not* leave my beautiful Emporium in that villain's hands."

Michael pushed his glasses up in the special way that showed he meant business. "We feel the same. But what do you propose?"

"Did your mother sign anything?"

Michael nodded. "That Gimble person brought something over this morning."

"Right. We find that paper, and we destroy it. Burn it! Chop it up! Eat it! Throw it in the river!" Montgomery waved his spoon around, chucking knickerbocker glory onto a smartly dressed lady at the next table. "If he's going to cheat, so can we."

"Do you know where he might keep it?" asked Michael.

"Of course. We met in his office, the first time."

Property was a bit startled by the idea of Eliot having an office. He had seemed to just appear from nowhere, like a shadow, or the plague.

"Right then," said Michael. "Let's go and get my mum's signature back."

"Splendid. *Splendid.* Are we agreed, young Property?"

Property hesitated. The memory of Eliot's face twitching in the half-light was still fresh, and she wasn't especially keen to run into him again. But she *did* want to beat him and win back the Emporium and the White Hart.

"All right," she said. She grinned at the others. "Let's do it." And the Gunther, with a baked bean on his nose, gave a warlike *MAWR.* So that settled *that.*

Pink and Gimble

Property was bubbling with impatience to get started, but there were two difficulties to deal with before they had even reached the office. First, there was still no sign of Netty. They waited a little, but she didn't reappear, and at last none of them could stand to wait any longer. In the end, Michael left a note at the bus stop to let her know that they were safe and would be back soon, and they went without her.

The second difficulty was worse. When they reached the corner of the little cobblestoned alleyway where Pink's office stood, they saw him walking toward them from the other end. They pulled back out of sight quickly.

"Curses," hissed Montgomery, "he must have got here another way. Quickly!"—and he hurried them into a shop across the road.

It turned out to be a hat shop. They spent an awkwardly long time in there, and the woman who ran it kept pestering them to try on hats, which was fair enough. They had to try on most of them twice because it wasn't a very big shop, and Montgomery ended up buying Michael a pinstripe top hat with a feather in it because the woman was getting so cross.

At last, Eliot reappeared. When he was a safe distance away, they hurried out of the shop and down the alley.

They stopped outside a gray door. It had a long window in it made of frosted glass—the kind that doesn't really let in any light—and a smart black knocker.

"Splendid, here we are, splendid," said Montgomery. "Ah—hmm. Does anybody know how to pick a lock?"

Property took out a hairpin and set to work. The door swung open with a slight squeak.

The room inside was dark, green, and lifeless. There was a small window, one desk piled high with papers, a second that was entirely bare, three large cabinets, and nothing else. Set in the far wall was a back door with another window, and through it Property could see a very overgrown garden.

"Right," said Michael, rolling up his sleeves. "Mr. Montgomery, could you keep watch? If they come, delay them as long as you can, and Prop and I will sneak out the back door. We'll meet back at the Café Splendide." Montgomery nodded and slipped out of the room.

Michael searched the papers on the desk, and Property searched the cabinets, the Gunther at her heels. She knew what Netty's signature looked like, so she didn't have to worry about her secret. The first cabinet was locked, with a fancy combination lock that she couldn't pick, and the second was empty apart from a couple of old coats. The third was full of shelves, all crammed with glass bottles. Blue inks and black inks and red inks. Dirty yellows and pale browns. Gold leaf and red wax. A jar full of licorice sticks. She spent a long time taking it all in.

"Well," said Michael, "it's not on the desk."

"Michael," said Property, "come and look at all this."

He came over to look. "Wow. This is amazing." He picked up a bottle of something thick and indigo that was kept between a bottle of something slightly lighter indigo and something slightly purple-ish indigo. "No labels on any of it," he remarked. "How does he know which one's which?"

"They look different," said Property, shrugging.

Just then, they heard voices outside. Eliot Pink was back—and Gimble too, by the sound of it.

Montgomery leapt into action and began telling the men a long-winded story about a miraculous recipe that he had invented for undoing lemonade stains. As he talked, Property and Michael crept to the back door and turned the handle. And turned it some more. They jiggled it. They tugged. They heaved.

No wonder the garden had looked unloved. The back door was stuck shut.

They could hear Montgomery listing ingredients, but his imagination wasn't very good, and they were getting more and more unlikely. Pink and Gimble finally lost patience at "mushy peas," and it sounded as if one of them picked Montgomery up and moved him out of the way. The key turned in the lock. Giving up on the door, Property gave Michael a shove toward the cabinet of old coats and scrambled in after him, the Gunther clinging tightly to her shoulder. Inside, they froze, hardly daring to breathe. The two men came into the room.

The cabinet was wonky and badly made. There was a crack between the doors that let Property see a sliver of the room. It turned out that a sliver was all she needed to see Gimble, who was a sliver of a man, short and slight. He was entirely hairless and eyebrow-less, with soft, puckered skin. He looked exactly like a finger in a suit.

"I don't like it," he was saying. "Why's Montgomery hanging around?"

"You worry too much, Gimble. He obviously doesn't know about the forgery." Eliot was out of sight, but his voice alone made Property's chest tighten.

"*You* never worry enough. I don't trust him. I don't trust any of them. I don't understand why you didn't silence those Joneses while you had the chance."

"Because I'm not rash, Gimble. There was no need."

"What if they interfere?"

"They won't. They're not the type," said Eliot. "And if they do, *then* I'll take care of them. No need to be hasty."

Property had an uncomfortable feeling that hiding in a cabinet probably counted as interfering. She breathed very, very quietly.

"Very well, very well," said Gimble, wriggling out of Property's line of vision. "Of course, if you hadn't *forgotten* to make mold marks—"

"For the last time, Montgomery would never have noticed. If it hadn't been for that obnoxious bookshop girl—"

"She's a little girl, Eliot, not a detective."

"She's exceptionally observant."

Gimble squirmed back into sight. His forehead was wrinkled, as if his eyebrows would be raised if he had any. "Oh, really? How fascinating. Does she have an extra eye? A microscope for a nose? Sensors in her fingertips?"

"Enough," growled Eliot. His tone made Property's heart somersault, but Gimble only smirked. "She's like me," said Eliot. "That's all."

"You mean she can't—?"

"Yes."

"But she lives in a bookshop."

"Yes."

"What kind of idiotic child lives in a bookshop and can't read?"

Property suddenly felt much too hot. She wished that she could see Michael's face, but she didn't dare move. Eliot didn't answer Gimble. There was a sticky silence.

"Oh, don't sulk," said Gimble, smirking more than ever. "I'm not saying *you're* an idiot. You know that I value your—ah—*special* relationship with books. There's no one else in the forgery business with such a good eye for faking papers and inks. Besides"—Gimble chuckled—"it's lucky for me. If you could read, you wouldn't need me to write the words, eh?"

No labels on Eliot's bottles, no papers on his desk.

He needed Gimble to handle his paperwork. He could have kept their beautiful bookshop, but instead he tore it apart for no good reason. And he had spotted Property's pretend-reading straight away, when the Joneses had never noticed. Property kicked herself for not realizing. Of course. Eliot couldn't read either.

He still wasn't talking to Gimble, but Gimble seemed happy to talk for both of them. "Anyway, enough—we'll put your little slipup behind us. Have you checked all the others? No more mistakes?"

"They're fine," Eliot growled.

"You've made me nervous. I just want to get all of these delivered and disappear. No trouble. Promise me you'll check them before they go out tomorrow? I wish I could be here. I don't like leaving it all to you. Are you listening to me, Eliot? Do you promise?"

"Yes. Would you like me to promise to brush my teeth and clean behind my ears as well?"

"Please don't be childish, Eliot. If we're going to pull this off, I need you to *think* for a minute. Two hundred forgeries to deliver in one day! These people are important, you know, and they're paying us a fortune. We can't afford mistakes."

Eliot slammed something down on a desk. "Don't question me. They're good."

"They'd better be." Gimble wriggled in delight. "This is our moment! It's going to make history! Every museum, every gallery, every rich, stupid so-and-so in the country is going to have one of our fakes."

"I know."

"We will be *so* outrageously rich this time tomorrow."

"I *know.* You never stop reminding me." But despite himself, Eliot sounded just a touch excited. "Have you got everything you need? We should get going."

"Oh, don't hurry me." Gimble was out of sight again, rustling through papers and rambling on about the important people that he was going to hoodwink. Something clicked to the left: Eliot was unlocking the other cabinet, looking for something. Property didn't even blink, praying that he wouldn't look in their cabinet.

His shadow fell across the crack between the doors. A long, gray coat was briefly visible. Then he moved on again. "Right," he said, "let's go."

Michael let out a tiny whimper of relief. The Gunther clamped his tail over Michael's mouth. They all waited.

Eliot turned. "Did you hear something?"

"No," said Gimble. "Now, have you definitely got the right book?"

Eliot grumbled in reply. Footsteps moved away. The door shut.

For ten seconds, no one moved. Then brother and sister and cat tumbled out of the cabinet in a heap of excited relief. Property ran to peer out of the window. There was no one in sight.

"Gone," she said.

"Good," said Michael. "Good, good, good."

MAWR, said the Gunther.

"Property," said Michael. He looked at her more properly than ever before. "What did he mean, about you? You can read. Can't you?"

The Joneses Interfere

Property wished that she was better at words. Michael would have known the words she needed. She wished she could tell him that it had not felt like pretending to sit and read with them, and that she hadn't set out to trick them. She wanted to explain that while she couldn't read the *letters*, there were stories in the cracks of the spine and the smell of the pages and the way the jacket feels under your fingers.

But she couldn't fit all of that into words. And besides, he hadn't asked. He had only asked whether she could read.

"No," she said. "Actually, I can't."

"Oh," said Michael.

Then Property said, "I'm so sorry I didn't tell you," and at the same time Michael said, "I'm so sorry I didn't realize."

"You've got nothing to be sorry for, Prop," said Michael.

"We should have thought of it. People aren't born knowing how to read. It's our fault."

Property didn't reply to that because there was a very large lump in her throat that was making it difficult to talk. It was also making it more difficult to pay attention. She didn't notice the two shadows through the frosted glass on the door, or the Gunther head-butting her ankles with more urgency than usual.

"Thanks, Michael," she said. And then there was a rap on the door, and with a sickening jolt, Property at last saw the figures outside. She froze.

The rap came again, and someone pressed their face against the door. "Michael? Prop?"

It was Netty with Montgomery.

Michael crumpled up a bit with relief and hurried to open the door and let them in. Netty hugged them both, and then Montgomery hugged them too, which was a bit awkward. "Oh dear, oh dear," he kept saying, "I thought something awful had happened! My dear young Joneses! Oh *dear.*"

Once they were satisfied that Michael and Property were both still in one piece, they had a hundred questions: "Where were you?" and "What happened?" and "Are you all right?" and "Why are you wearing a top hat, love?" and "Well, my dear Joneses, did you find those papers?"

The papers! Property had almost forgotten why they were there. Her brain scrambled to get back to business. She had heard Eliot unlocking the last cabinet—the only place they hadn't looked. While Michael was explaining what had happened, tactfully avoiding Property's secret, Property tried the cabinet door. It was still unlocked. She pulled it open, willing it to have Netty's signature waiting inside.

The cabinet very obviously didn't contain any fresh, new papers. It was so beautiful, though, that Property forgot to be disappointed. It was full of ancient-looking books. Some of them were beautifully gilded or bound in soft leather or stitched up with silk. Others were thin and fragile, and some were even just single tattered sheets, covered in urgent, spikey writing. They looked so full of secrets that Property *wished* she could read them.

"What's that you've found, Prop?" said Netty. The others crowded round to look. Montgomery's eyes bulged.

"My goodness," he breathed. "King Arthur...da Vinci... Saint Augustine...Christopher Columbus...Julius Caesar... My *goodness...*"

"Don't get excited," said Michael. "They're all fakes." He ran a finger down some of the spines. "They've got every celebrity in history here. They're going to make a fortune."

"This is what Michael was telling you about. Pink and Gimble's big job," said Property. "We were just a practice. They won't even need our money this time tomorrow, when they sell all of these." She fought the urge to tear all the forgeries apart. That would probably count as inter-fering, and it wouldn't actually help.

Montgomery had pulled one of the books from the top of a shelf and was leafing through it. "I have to say, these are impressive. I'd never have guessed this color-ing was licorice. And the writing—this *must* have been done with a real quill. That scoundrel really does get the details just right."

"It's not *that* impressive," said Property. "He just pays attention, that's all. It's not like he did the words."

And it was then that Property had a good idea. In fact, it was a very good idea. But it was a bit extraordinary, so she had to think about it for a few seconds before she was sure.

It would *definitely* count as interfering. But it just might work.

"Wait," she said. "If two hundred of the most important museums and galleries and libraries all complain that they've been sold a forgery, then people will have to listen, won't they?"

Netty nodded. "Sure. But not everyone's as observant as you, love. Unless they all figure it out very quickly, Pink will be able to disappear."

"Right," said Property. "So, I reckon we need to make it really, really obvious for them. We need to make sure that they all complain straight away."

The others blinked at her uncertainly, and the Gunther, now desperate to leave, had started nibbling at her feet and yowling sadly. But Property was warming to her very good idea, and she wasn't going to be put off.

"Look, Eliot's the only one here tomorrow, and Eliot can't read. As long as they *look* right, he won't know what they actually *say*. Why don't we add a few words of our own?" She looked at the bottles of ink, winking at her in the light. "We'd need to use the right inks, or he'd notice. I reckon I'd be good at that. And I'm sure that you could all come up with great things to write. As soon as people *read* their precious books, they'll be demanding an explanation."

Michael grinned at her. "Ha! Yep, I can think of a few words that King Arthur *definitely* never wrote..."

"Exactly!"

"But Michael said that there are two hundred of them," said Albert H. Montgomery. "If we can add something to all of them in one night, it will be a miracle."

Property smiled. "An Object of Wonder. They do happen sometimes, you know."

"What if they come back?" asked Netty.

Property didn't have an answer to this. "I don't know," she admitted. "But we can't just leave and do nothing. It's not just about us now. They're going to bankrupt every bookshop and library in the country with these!"

"Come on, Mum, we *have* to try," said Michael. And although the others *umm*ed and *aah*ed nervously, they felt the same, and it didn't take long to persuade them. Besides, as soon as they started coming up with ideas for unlikely things for the kings and queens and poets and saints and philosophers to write, they were laughing so much that they all felt a bit giddy. It was too tempting not to try.

So Netty and Montgomery sat at the two desks, and Michael sat under one of them, and all three started dreaming up a list of unlikely phrases. The Gunther kept lookout at the window. He wasn't great at this because he kept stopping to have angry fights with his tail, but at least it kept him out of everyone's way.

Meanwhile, Property got to know the inks. Dark blue and navy and indigo, pitch black and shadow black and midnight black, rust red and brick red and terra-cotta, all glistening and glooping in their bottles. Then there were the dip-pens and quills, all shaped differently for spikier or fatter or smoother writing. Property fished some paper out of a bin and tried them out, comparing the results to the piles of fake books.

She found that the inks looked different depending which paper they were used on. And there was the problem of their different smells and the way that some of them changed color as they dried. She had to get it exactly right. Eliot would be sure to spot any mistakes.

Once she was sure that she had found a match, she would pass the book, ink, and pen to one of the others, and they would add in some words of their own. After the first rush of ideas and excited giggling had calmed down, they worked silently, apart from the scratching of pens. They had to write very carefully, and it was slow work. For a long time, the mountain of unfinished books didn't seem to get any smaller.

They worked until the sky outside smudged first into dusk, and then into dark, at which point they turned on a feeble light. At night, the White Hart had always been cozy, and the Emporium was huge and majestic in the darkness, but the office of Pink and Gimble just felt drab.

Property was suddenly struck by the thought that having Eliot Pink's brain would be like being stuck inside this room: nothing comfortable or interesting or beautiful, nothing really alive, just cupboards full of clever schemes. She paused with her pen in midair, taken aback by the thought. If this was true, she wouldn't want to be Eliot Pink if he had a *hundred* book emporiums. She shook off the thought with a shudder and got back to work.

Her second sleepless night in a row made her feel very peculiar. Sometimes she forgot where she was or why she was doing this and would just get lost inside the scratching of the pens and the glittering ribbons of ink. Then the Gunther would helpfully nibble her toes to wake her up again.

The others were a little more awake, but the night still took its toll. By the time they reached the last book, supposedly by Robin Hood, their brains had given in.

"*Uuuh,*" Michael said. "Er. Does anyone else have any

ideas? I'm thinking I'll just write I LIKE BANANAS in really big letters."

The Gunther crossed his eyes and blew a raspberry.

"Tell your charming cat," said Michael, "that Robin Hood would never have seen bananas. We didn't have them in Britain in those days. So it's actually a *great* idea." And he yawned widely enough to swallow the room.

It wasn't one of Michael's better ideas, but birds were singing outside by now, so they all told him it was very clever. When he had finished, Property put the book back in the cabinet, stoppered up the inks, put them away, and looked around the room. Apart from a few thousand new words, everything was just as they had found it.

"Well done, everyone, well done," said Netty. "Let's get out of here."

And so they did. Property turned off the light on the way out, and four shadows hurried away from the offices of Pink and Gimble. The smallest shadow appeared to have a cat for a head, which would have confused passersby if there had been any. But no one saw them. By the time London woke up, the Joneses and their cat were tucked up in Montgomery's house, to wait and see whether their *interference* had worked.

And while they waited, they all had a *very* good day's sleep.

Chapter Nine

A Very Important Mob

Montgomery's family was away at his "little place in the country," so Property was staying in one of the children's rooms. The bed had heavy velvet blankets, which made her all hot and bothered. She missed her hammock.

Montgomery kept watch on the office that day and reported back to the Joneses when they woke up. Eliot had left the office with some large, black briefcases, Montgomery said; the rest had been taken away in a van. It didn't look as if Eliot had noticed anything wrong. Now there was nothing to do but wait for the very important people to read their books.

Property found the waiting unbearable. First, she couldn't shake off the feeling that Eliot might have somehow outsmarted them. Second, Michael wouldn't stop hinting that she should tell Netty about the whole not-being-able-to-read situation. Property hinted right back that Michael should mind his own business. But he wouldn't let it drop.

The next morning, the wait was over. Montgomery came running back from his spying mission while they were all still at breakfast. "Come and see, come and see!" he panted, waving an excited hand and knocking over the teapot. The cold tea soaked the Gunther, whose ears instantly turned inside out in shock, but Montgomery didn't notice. "It's splendid! It's magnificent! Hurry, hurry!"

So they abandoned their cornflakes and hurried out, Property wrapping the Gunther in her scarf to dry. They half-ran all the way. (They would have fully-run, but they hadn't finished their breakfast. Nobody can be expected to run without a proper breakfast inside them.)

In the alley there was a swarm of people, who all looked very important and very annoyed. Montgomery and the Joneses elbowed their way toward the front to see what was going on.

In the doorway stood a nervous police officer, who was tugging at his mustache and looking a bit overwhelmed by the whole situation. Property nudged Michael and pointed at the window. Gimble's panicked face was pressed against the glass. Eliot stood behind him, scowling.

"Ladies and gentlemen, *please*," said the officer. "I can only listen to your complaints one at a time."

The ladies and gentlemen ignored this enthusiastically. All these things were shouted at the same time:

"Bring them out here!"

"We demand *justice*!"

"I paid twenty-three million pounds for this!"

"They're making fun of us!"

"This is supposed to be Latin poetry," roared a jewel-covered woman, "but I translated the first page, and it's just 'The Incy Wincy Spider.' And *incius wincius* isn't even real Latin."

Behind her, a bearded man was yelling, "And even if King Alfred the Great *did* have smelly feet, I'm sure he wouldn't have written to the Pope about it. Or asked him to pray for his socks."

"This letter," thundered a ketchup-colored man, "claims that Cleopatra had a pet T. rex called Nigel!"

"Really?" said the man next to him. "That's interesting. My name's Nigel. Strange name for a T. rex, though."

The ketchup-colored man shook with anger. "She didn't *really* have a T. rex, you *NINCOMPOOP*!"

"All right," said Nigel. "Calm down."

"This Greek tragedy ends with a recipe for angel food cake!" someone at the front screeched. Montgomery smiled.

A nervous-looking man next to Property cleared his throat. "I don't want to be awkward," he explained, "but I just don't think that Robin Hood would have *seen* a banana." And then it was Michael's turn to smile.

The din grew louder and louder. "It's a scandal!" "It's an outrage!" "They're mocking us all!" "They're taking us for fools!" "*MAWR!*" Those nearest the front were banging on the office door. The ketchup-colored man was by now wrestling Nigel. The police officer had a go at hiding behind his hat.

"We want our money back!" roared the bearded man. And then the whole crowd took up the chant, until they were so loud that it felt as if the alley must surely burst with the sound.

The officer tugged at his mustache, cleared his throat, and tugged at the other side of his mustache. None of which helped. In the end he said, "One moment, please," and ducked back into the office, slamming the door behind him. He could be seen through the window, arguing with Gimble. It didn't look like Eliot was saying much.

At length, the officer emerged again, looking determined. This was a bit like watching a beetle get tough with a pack of hyenas.

"Ladies and gentlemen," he said—and then he said it again, louder—and then he shouted it so loudly that his mustache rippled: "LADIES AND GENTLEMEN. I have spoken to Mr. Gimble and Mr. Pink. They are very sorry for the—ah, mistakes." (Behind him, through the window, Gimble could be seen shouting at Eliot. Eliot was ignoring him thunderously. Neither of them *looked* especially sorry.) "I am pleased to say," the policeman continued, "that they are willing to pay you all back immediately."

There was an uproarious cheer. "Of course they are, the rogues," muttered Montgomery. "Either they pay or it's prison for both of them."

"SO," bellowed the officer, "please form an orderly line to make your claims. ONE AT A TIME. And then please go away. Quietly. Please."

With much elbowing and shoving, the very important mob became a very important line. The officer opened the door, and one by one they all filed in. The Joneses waited too. Property's heart was pounding. It had really worked!

At last it was their turn. When they approached the

desk, Eliot's face twitched all over, and his lips grew very thin. He didn't look at Property.

"Hello," said Michael cheerfully. "We bought a Shakespeare play, but where it should say 'by William Shakespeare' it says 'by Sillythem Fake-here.'"

"No, it doesn't," said Eliot.

"For the last time, Mr. Pink," said the officer, "if you don't want to be arrested, you will be *helpful.*"

"We paid with everything we have, including two bookshops," said Netty. "I want my signature back."

Gimble looked to Eliot. Eliot looked, at last, at Property. He looked at her hands. Property looked too and realized that there were still some ink stains on her fingers. It didn't prove anything—pens leak all the time—but she could see that *he* knew. She shoved her hands in her pockets and stared at him without blinking.

"Well, Mr. Pink?" said the officer. He glanced at the Joneses nervously, as if he was worried that they might cause a riot. (To be fair, the Gunther was looking pretty ready to riot, but he was just getting ready to have a fight with the officer's mustache.)

Eliot fished in his pockets and pulled out the papers. He handed them over.

"This," he spat, "is cheating."

"Gosh," replied Property quietly. "So it is."

The officer didn't hear her, because he was busy adding the Joneses' complaint to a long list. Here are some of the things he had written:

Evidence of book forgeries sold by Mr. E. Pink and Mr. N. Gimble:
   —Sacred book by 12th-century monk is mostly the opening to Star Wars
   —Map of Ancient Egypt is actually map of Swindon
   —Ancient philosopher Aristotle claims that the meaning of life is deep-dish pizza
   —Book of Roman law says that on Friday nights, all Romans must get down and boogie to the funky beats

He now added:
   —Stupid name for Shakespeare
   —Complainants: Ms., Mr., & Miss Jones; Mr. Montgomery; Something that is probably a cat

"Right," he said, "Was there anything else?"

"No thanks," said Michael. He beamed at them. "We've got everything we could possibly need."

And this, thought Property, was true.

Chapter Ten

The Great Jones Book Emporium

When Montgomery, the Joneses, and the Gunther returned to the Emporium, the Wollups were still packing it up. The armchairs and lamps had gone from the shop floor. It was almost bare.

Montgomery turned a little pale. He stopped the nearest Wollup. "Who," he demanded, "are you?"

The Wollup looked at him mournfully. "Wollup," he said. "I just work for Pink," he said. "That's all," he added, sighing.

"I doubt that you do work for him anymore, you know," said Montgomery. "The police are in his office right now. He's going to be driven out of business."

"Oh." The Wollup turned this idea over in his mind. Something like a smile crept across his face.

"And he doesn't own this Emporium anymore," Montgomery went on, "so I'm sorry to trouble you, but we're going to have to ask you to put everything back."

The Wollup sighed. It was the deep sigh of a man who has to spend today undoing yesterday's work and isn't even surprised, because deep down he suspects that this might be what life is all about.

Montgomery produced a bottle of lemonade from under the counter and poured them all a celebratory glass. He raised his in the air, spilling a little on the way. "To the Great Jones Book Emporium!"

The Joneses raised their glasses too, a little uncertainly. "Mr. Montgomery," said Michael. "Don't you—er. We were wondering. Don't you want it back now?" Property could see that it pained Michael to even ask the question. He had fallen in love with the Emporium from the moment that they arrived.

"No, no," said Montgomery, "I really think I would like to retire. I've been thinking that I'll open a cozy little library somewhere quiet. Get back to the books. It's all got a bit much for me here, since the business took off—I'm not really cut out to be a businessman. As you've seen."

That was when Property had her second very good idea.

"You could use our old bookshop for your library," she said. "It's really cozy, and we're not using it."

"That," said Montgomery, "sounds like a splendid idea."

And they all drank another toast, this time to the White Hart Library and all its cupboards.

Michael asked hopefully whether the Gunther might go to the White Hart with Montgomery, but the kitten dug all his claws into Property's shoulder and tied his tail around her ear. So that answered *that* question. Montgomery looked a little bit relieved.

"I'm sure you'll all do splendidly here," he said. "And may I say, my dear Joneses, that I cannot think of anyone more deserving of this Emporium. Your achievements since you got here have been magnificent."

"It was all Property, really," said Netty.

"Yes, she's brilliant," said Michael. He nudged Property and raised his eyebrows. "And we'll always think she's brilliant, *no matter what.*"

"Thanks," said Property. She ignored the hint.

"If she ever wanted to *tell us anything*," said Michael, nudging so hard that he dislodged the Gunther, "there is absolutely no way that we would ever be angry about it."

Montgomery and Netty nodded, but they looked a bit confused. Property rubbed her sore arm.

"In fact," said Michael, "now would be a great time for us to all talk about anything that was bothering us. *I* think."

"All right, *all right*," said Property. She took a deep breath. She accidentally breathed in the Gunther's tail. There was an awkward bit of coughing. Then she said, "Mum. I can't read. I'm sorry I didn't say anything. I didn't know what you were both doing at first. And then I was too scared to tell you. And then it just didn't seem worth mentioning. But now I think I'd like to learn, please."

Netty's face did something that Property had only seen once before. It was the same expression that she had made on finding a five-year-old girl in her lost property cupboard. It was an expression that seemed to say, "Well, this is very surprising, but the only thing to do is to be sensible about it."

"Well then," she said at last, "we will have to teach you."

Property couldn't find the right words, as usual. So she hugged Netty very hard, and the Gunther licked her face and patted her nose with his paw, and that got the general message across.

There was an almighty crunch behind them as a Wollup turned a stack. It was, Property saw, the Room of Sticky Endings, which had finally unstuck itself. She smiled. The Emporium was starting to look a little more like its old self. The armchairs and lamps were back out, the woodland creatures had been released from their crate, and the first of the books were back on the shelves.

It was good to see it come back to life. It could never replace the White Hart, thought Property, but it *was* an Object of Wonder.

They do happen, sometimes.

Before We Finish

So that is the story of Property Jones, and now you have heard all of it. But people always have questions, of course. So before we finish it, I will answer a few.

What happened to Pink and Gimble? Gimble became some sort of small-time lawyer, who can still be seen squirming around the shabbier parts of London. But Eliot Pink walked away the next day, down a long, gray road out of town, and he hasn't been seen since.

The more kindhearted readers sometimes want to know what happened to the Wollups. I am happy to report that they made themselves so useful, putting the Emporium back together double-quick, that the Joneses decided to hire them. Now they are all booksellers, and they look like a much happier sort of walrus. They have even made friends with the Gunther, which is just as well, because he has grown much bigger and no less fierce.

Some people ask who Property's real family was. To those people, I say: the Joneses. There is nothing more to be said about *that*.

And lastly, of course: did Property ever learn to read? She did. She was not especially good at it, and it took her a long time. But she had a whole Book Emporium to choose from—not to mention a library, which she visited every weekend to drink lemonade with the librarian—so she got there in the end.

She quite liked reading books, on the whole. She didn't like saying goodbye to the characters at the end, but she knew that "goodbye" only means "God be with you," and she came back to her favorites as often as she wanted. They were always waiting for her.

And she *did* like the sound that a book makes when you shut it: a very, very tiny *thmph*.

Like shutting a door that is barely there at all.

Acknowledgments

As Property understands well, a book is not just the words on the page. There are many people who have provided the inspiration, encouragement, experiences, and tea, which are as much a part of this story as the commas and full stops are.

Huge thanks go to three wonderful draft-readers and friends: Sam Plumb, Dylan Townley, and Erin Simmons. Thanks also to my two excellent editors, Lucy Rogers and Genevieve Herr, for their wise words and support. Lucy is responsible for the arrival of a cat in this tale, so blame the Gunther on her. And a big thank-you to Olivia Horrox and all the team at Scholastic who have helped *The Bookshop Girl* make its way into the world.

Finally, thanks always to Bryony Woods, agent extraordinaire.

You are all the bee's knees.

Q&A with Sylvia Bishop

Where do you get your ideas?

I think ideas are everywhere. We only run into trouble when we worry about finding a good idea, because as soon as we do that we start criticizing all our ideas before they can even get started. Anything that I find funny or magical or exciting could be a funny, magical, or exciting story, and the trick is to try writing about all of them with an open mind and see what happens.

I think we all see things that appeal to us every day. And if it appeals to you, it will appeal to someone else, and it could be a story.

Property's secret is that she can't read. Did you love reading as a child? What were your favorite books growing up?

I did love to read, but I think I would still have got on well with Property, because I also liked the books themselves. I liked hardbacks and thick pages and beautiful pictures. I loved the Winnie-the-Pooh books, because they are so funny, and my father would read them to me with all the right voices. Later I loved everything by Diana Wynne Jones, who writes about wonderfully detailed, interesting magical worlds. And *A Little Princess*, by Frances Hodgson Burnett, was a firm favorite.

Where do you write? Do you have a special place?

I wrote *The Bookshop Girl* at my desk in Oxford, with my red Anglepoise lamp. Now I've moved to London, but the desk and the lamp have come with me, so when I sit down to write it's as though I never left.

That's how I like to write best—at my desk, first thing in the morning or last thing at night. But sometimes life gets in the way, and the wonderful thing about writing is that you can do it anywhere, anytime.

What do you think happened next for Property and her family?

I don't know, and I think it's very important that I don't know. You, reading this book, have invented a whole new version of Property and Netty and Michael and the White Hart and the Great Montgomery Book Emporium. The version of this story that now lives inside your head is uniquely yours and not quite like mine or anyone else's. So if you want to know what happens next, you have as much right to dream up an answer as I do. That is the wonderful thing about stories.

Do you have more fun writing good characters or bad characters?

I think I like best the challenge of trying to write people who aren't quite one or the other, or aren't what they seem. In this book, Montgomery did the right thing in the end, but he messed up at first— oh, but for good reasons, poor man! I think readers will disagree about how well we should think of Montgomery. And I enjoy that. That's how real people are—confusing! And it's fun to try to capture that in writing.

About the Author

Sylvia Bishop spent her entire childhood reading fiction, dreaming up stories, and pretending. She then tried very hard to come to grips with the real world by studying politics and going into social science research. She lives in London.

sylviabishopbooks.weebly.com

About the Illustrator

Poly Bernatene studied drawing and painting at the Buenos Aires School of Fine Art. As well as working in animation and comics, he has illustrated over sixty children's books. He lives in Argentina.

www.polybernatene.com